The SHONN Project

Books in the
Perimeter One Adventures series

The SHONN Project

DAVID WARD

OLIVER
NELSON

THOMAS NELSON PUBLISHERS
Nashville • Atlanta • London • Vancouver

Published in Nashville, Tennessee, by Thomas Nelson, Inc., Publishers, and distributed in Canada by Word Communications, Ltd., Richmond, British Columbia.

The Bible version used in this publication is THE NEW KING JAMES VERSION. Copyright © 1979, 1980, 1982, Thomas Nelson, Inc., Publishers.

Library of Congress Cataloging-in-Publication Data

Ward, David, 1961–
    The SHONN project / David Ward.
        p.   cm. — (Perimeter One adventure series : bk. 2)
    Summary: Chris Graham, a student at a science academy on one of Jupiter's moons, becomes involved in a secret project to build a sentient humanoid, not knowing that the device is intended for destruction.
    ISBN 0-8407-9236-0
    [1. Robots—Fiction.   2. Science fiction.]   I. Title.
II. Series: Ward, David. 1961–   Perimeter One adventures series : bk. 2.
PZ7.W1873Sh   1994
[Fic]—dc20   94–10516
                                                                    CIP
                                                                     AC

Printed in the United States of America.
1 2 3 4 5 6 — 99 98 97 96 95 94

Prologue

As night fell, a shadowy figure scaled the grassy knoll to the converter station and stole along the low brick building. Light shone on him briefly as he passed quickly by one of the windows, revealing a man dressed in black wearing a mask. The mask was clear plastic, molded to the contours of his face, but the face underneath was covered in black so that no features were discernable.

He walked slowly along the wall of the building until he found what he was looking for—a grate nearly overgrown by the surrounding grass. The grate was mounted with reverse locking screws to prevent tampering with a screwdriver. He removed a small vial of acid from his utility belt and poured a few drops on the head of each screw. The hiss was loud enough to attract attention, but when he looked around, he was still alone.

The screws melted, he lifted the grate easily to one side and dropped down into the opening. According to the plans he had studied, the passage was a ventilation duct that had been out of service since the converter station became operational. His small hand torch lit the tunnel ahead, and he moved gingerly into the darkness. The condensation inside his mask made it difficult to see.

After a few minutes, he came to a dead end. Beyond the wall came a deep hum; the walls and the floor were vibrating now. The man's breathing was short and labored. If he were going to turn back, it would be now or never.

He squared his shoulders with resolve and pulled a black box off his belt, placing it on the floor against the wall. The device contained a laser, precisely adjusted for the composition of the wall. Equipped with adhesive wheels, the box climbed the wall with surprising speed, cutting a rectangle three feet high and two feet across. The man put the device back on his belt and used a pair of suction cups with handles to remove the makeshift doorway. As the section came free of the wall, the hum became deafening. Just beyond the hole was a large generator. He stepped through and found just enough space to move with his back flattened to the wall.

Once clear of the generator, he found himself in a cavernous chamber filled with huge and varied pieces of machinery. Using a scrap of paper as his guide, he made his way to the nearest logic conduit and opened the panel.

He removed a set of tiny tools and soiled booklet from his belt and went to work. Sweat from his forehead mingled with the condensation inside his mask until water dripped from the eyeholes, making it hard to see. *One bad connection,* he thought, *and the automatic alarms go off.* Several minutes later, he pulled several pieces from the logic conduit, stowed them in a cloth bag at his waist, and closed the panel. He hurried out the way he had come in, carefully replacing the section of the wall and the grate, and disappeared into the shadows.

CHAPTER 1

 "Queen to rook two. Checkmate."

"Nice game. Do you want to play again?"

"No."

Ryan Graham usually enjoyed playing chess against his desktop computer, but this was the third game he'd won this morning. There was no longer any challenge.

"I better find a new opponent and quick," he said, thinking out loud. "The championship tournament is next week."

"Sorry, but I did not understand that," the computer responded.

He switched off the computer and put the chess board on the top shelf above the desk. He was becoming tall for his age, having grown two inches in three months since his sixteenth birthday. He was good-looking, with dark brown hair and brown eyes, but he had an easy smile and a quick wit that kept him from taking himself too seriously.

He was looking for his shoes when his mom called upstairs. "Ryan! Breakfast! You'll be late for school."

"I can't find my shoes."

"Did you look under that pile of clothes at the end of your bed?"

He checked and, of course, she was right.

"I hate it when she's right," he said under his breath with a hint of a smile. It occurred to him that she always seemed to know when he'd been in the cookie jar, too. "How do moms know this stuff?" He shook his head and charged out of his room, nearly knocking his sister over.

"Whoops! Sorry," Ryan said, not even breaking stride. He grabbed the newel post at the top of the bannister, swinging around and down the stairs, even though his father had told him not to do so a hundred times. Miraculously, the railing held.

With all the outrage she could muster, Amie put her fists on her hips and tossed back her auburn hair, brown eyes flashing. "Don't worry," she said to the back of his head as he reached the landing. "I'm sure my foot will recover. That's why God gave me two!"

"Good thing He didn't give you two mouths!" Ryan shot back, disappearing down the next flight of stairs.

The Grahams lived in a townhouse on King Street, in Arlington, Virginia, a ten-minute ground-car commute from downtown Washington, D.C. The house was long and narrow, with five floors and a tiny backyard surrounded by a brick wall. Because of the convenient location, the house had changed hands with every new government administration, so the list of prior owners included a number of famous people.

Ryan hit the main floor and slid into the kitchen. The smell of bacon was wonderful. He took the chair next to his dad, who was drinking his decaf and reading the morning news. Dr. Nathan Graham was almost fifty, with only a sprinkling of gray in his dark hair and well-groomed mustache.

His wife, Millie, was the same age as he, although she would never admit it unless you asked. Her dark brown hair also was tinged with gray, but her dark brown eyes sparkled with fun. At the moment she was stirring something wonderful in a large pan.

"What's for breakfast?" Ryan asked, thinking *Bacon! Bacon! Bacon!*

"Garbage. Say good morning to your father."

"Hi, Dad."

Nathan put down his paper. "Good morning, Ryan. How are you?"

Ryan forgot about the bacon for a moment. "Discouraged."

"Discouraged? Well, so am I. What's your excuse?"

"The chess tournament is next week and I don't think I'm ready."

"Why?"

"I beat the computer three times this morning. It was too easy."

"Why don't you play your mother?"

"Nah. She always makes those weird moves."

"Who usually wins?"

Ryan couldn't argue with that. "Hey, Mom? What do you say?"

"Right now, I say it's time for you to eat and get yourself to school. We'll discuss it when you get home."

Amie walked in and kissed her father on the cheek. "Hi, Daddy. Hi, Mom."

Millie offered her cheek and was rewarded with a kiss. She put plates of food before each of them and sat down. They held hands and said a brief prayer for the day, and then Nathan pulled a card out of a small ceramic cup and read a Scripture verse.

"'If we confess our sins, He is faithful and just to forgive us our sins and to cleanse us from all unrighteousness.' Any guesses?"

Ryan took a stab at it. "John four-sixteen?"

"Nice try. But no."

Amie put her napkin in her lap. "Romans eight-twenty-eight?"

"Sorry. Millicent, dear?"

Millie hated being called that, and they all knew the only thing saving Nathan from certain death was the "dear" tacked on the end. Millie smiled sweetly. "First John one-nine."

"Correct. You've been doing your homework."

"Actually, it was the sermon text last Sunday."

Nathan was somewhat abashed. He hadn't been paying close attention that particular Sunday. "Oh. Yes. Of course it was."

Ryan wolfed down the rest of his breakfast, kissed his folks on the cheek, and shot out the door and up the stairs.

"Slow down there, Speedy!" Nathan hollered. "You're supposed to walk your sister to the bus stop."

"Well, tell her to hurry up!"

Millie patted her daughter gently on the knee. "Better go, sweetie."

Amie took one more bite of toast, grabbed her coat and her books, and headed for the front door. "I'm coming."

"Good luck on the show!" Millie yelled after her.

As the front door closed behind them, Nathan picked the newspaper back up. "Amie's tryouts were yesterday?"

"Yes. The cast list should be posted this morning." Millie sat down next to her husband. "Did I hear you say you were discouraged?"

"Yes."

"What's your excuse?"

"Well, I'm not really discouraged. Mostly bored, I think. The most exciting thing we've had at work in the last six weeks is some solar flare activity."

"Sometimes it's like that."

"I know. I'd rather be busy, that's all."

"Something will turn up. It always does."

As Ryan and Amie walked down the driveway, they saw the bus had already stopped at the corner. Without a word they broke into a dead run. Fortunately, the driver saw them and waited with the door open. They dashed up the steps and found seats on different sides of the bus, studiously ignoring each other.

Amie struck up a conversation with her seatmate and good friend, Penny DeShappelle, over the dull roar of conversation on the bus. "What did you think of tryouts yesterday?"

"Wild. You think I have a shot at the part of Maria?" Penny asked. Between the noise on the bus, Penny's trademark wad of chewing gum, and the fact that she talked ninety miles an hour, she had to repeat herself twice before Amie understood her.

"Same shot as anyone else. You got more guts than I do."

"What part did you try out for?"

"Anita." Amie effected a Hispanic accent. "Puerto Rico. . . ."

"Oh, you'd be perfect!"

The bus arrived at the school a short time later, and Ryan was the first one off. He walked through the quadruple doors into the circular commons beyond and turned left toward his locker.

Amie came off the bus dead last, still chattering away with Penny. The two of them headed straight to the drama room, pressing through the crowd trying to see the cast list posted on the door.

The route to Ryan's locker always took him by a large plaque listing honors graduates for the last five years. One third of the way down was his brother's name. Chris Graham had graduated with high honors two years earlier and had chosen to attend the Space Sciences Academy. Ryan had long ago quit trying to compete with his brother. In the past year, his teachers had mercifully given up the annoying comparisons. Chris was an *A* student, but Ryan could still beat his pants off in chess.

He had just opened his locker when Amie came running up. "I got a lead in the play!"

For an instant, all else was forgotten. Ryan grinned from ear to ear and gave her a bear hug. "Good job! You gotta call Mom and tell her."

He slammed his locker shut and the two of them walked off in search of a communicator. Ryan was really proud of his little sister, and for the moment, he didn't care who saw them together.

By all appearances it was a typical college dorm room. The long walls showed a mirror image of matching closets, sofa beds, and desks down the sides. The large window at the end of the room was open slightly and a gentle breeze blew, smelling of freshly cut grass. The view was really quite lovely. The campus had been designed to rest in a valley of broad green fields with lush, wooded hills all around. This particular room was on the third floor and so had a clear view across campus of the Science Hall, the Humanities Center, and the Student Union Building, or SUB as it was known to the students.

A ten-minute walk to the top of one of the surrounding hills would have revealed the dazzling vista an illusion. On the other side stood a nearly invisible wall, and what looked like sky overhead was actually a dome. Fashioned from a combination of advanced polymers and mimetic display technology, the dome could simulate night and day and give the illusion of the change of seasons as well. The dome had been formed as a single piece in space and attached to the supporting structure before the whole construction was carefully lowered into place.

Outside the dome was the tortured surface of Io, a Jovian moon with no layer of atmosphere to protect it. Io was about the same size as Earth's moon, with crimson rivers of molten rock, calderas, and volcanos creating a constant, silent maelstrom of volcanic activity all the way to the horizon and beyond. Overhead, against the star-studded pitch blackness of space, the gigantic sphere of Jupiter dominated the view.

Three decades earlier, the scientific community on Earth had decided to build a Space Sciences Academy on one of Jupiter's moons because of the opportunities for study provided by such a location. Io was chosen primarily because the geothermal energy located so near the surface could be used to power the entire facility. The only problem that remained was finding a safe place to build. Exhaustive studies pinpointed the most stable spot, and in the end the academy averaged only five major moonquakes a year, none of them serious enough to challenge the construction of the dome.

Actually, there were tremors almost daily, but most people got used to them in the first week or so. The fixtures and furniture inside the dome were equipped with special adhesive and fasteners so that free-standing objects could be anchored at a moment's notice. The biggest problem was the occasional overachiever who ignored the tremor warning lights mounted overhead and continued studying. Once or twice a month one of these students spent an hour or so sorting his or her papers and books back in a usable order.

Tremors or no, new arrivals to the academy were always relieved to walk into such a beautiful setting after the long flight cooped up in a spaceship. The computer-generated sunlight overhead was only eighty percent as bright as Earth's sun, but without a view from Earth as comparison, it was impossible to tell the difference.

Another breeze wafted through the dorm window, bringing a small housefly with it. The fly buzzed noisily across the surface of the glass, pausing as if to make sure the surface was really impenetrable.

Over one desk hung a cork bulletin board belonging to Chris Graham, peppered with family pictures. There, to the left, was the whole family at their home back on Earth. The photo had been taken in summer, just before Chris, at eighteen, had begun his third year at the academy.

The door opened suddenly and in strode Chris with an armload of books. He walked briskly to his desk and dropped them. At one-sixth of Earth's gravity, they appeared to fall in slow motion and hit the desk rather more softly than they ought. He kicked off his loafers, shed his clothes like a man on fire, and threw on an old T-shirt and some running shorts.

He was looking for his athletic shoes when the fly landed on the side of his head and tickled his right ear. He ducked, took a swing, missed, swung, and missed a second time. The fly beat a hasty retreat to the opposite wall, no doubt planning its next assault.

Chris reached down slowly and picked up his notebook, balancing it carefully on the palm of his hand. He slowly drew a breath, eyeing his assailant warily. "Nice fly . . . good fly. Hold still. I have some light reading for you."

With a deft flick of his wrist, the notebook flew across the room and smashed the fly flat against the wall. He used a facial tissue to wipe the wall clean and then began poking through

7

the insect's remains with a straight pin. *If Amie were here, she would run from the room screaming,* he thought to himself.

He soon found what he was looking for—a tiny transmitter that had stopped working upon its brief encounter with the notebook. He picked up the device with a pair of tweezers and carefully placed it in a small plastic box with a half dozen others. He had been hoping to do some reverse engineering on these doodads to see how they worked. The biology students were notoriously tightfisted with their secrets.

All animal, plant, and insect life inside the dome had to be carefully regulated to maintain a balance, so there were powerful computers in the zoology, entomology, and botany labs designed to monitor life signs and make adjustments as necessary. Even now, one of the machines was hard at work breeding a replacement for Chris's most recent victim.

He had just resumed the search for his shoes when he heard a familiar voice outside.

"Hey, Gramface! Get a move on. We've got a game to win!"

Chris threw the window open wide and looked down into the impatient face of Emmanuel Hascome, or Manny for short, his best friend and roommate. Manny had short, dark hair and an olive complexion.

"Salutations, Manfred, but I can't find my shoes."

"Did you look under your clothes?"

Chris turned around and lifted a pile of dirty laundry at the end of his bed, and sure enough, there were his shoes. He slipped them on and pushed a spot above each heel. The shoes sealed snugly around his feet, ready to provide additional support in response to angular stress.

He stood up and without a second thought yelled, "Incoming!" Then he vaulted the bookshelf and sailed out the window, dropping thirty feet to the ground below. Even with the gravity adjustment, he still hit hard. Manny had to twist violently out of the way to avoid disaster.

"Hey, watch it!"

Chris stood up and Manny looked down.

"They were right where I said, weren't they?" he said smugly. They started walking.

"You know me too well, Scummy."

Manny winced. "Do you have to call me that?"

"It's not my fault your last name ends with 'scum.' Still not shaving, I see."

"I want to look mean for our game."

Chris eyed him appraisingly. "Well, scruffy will get you half-way there, but you'll have to do the rest."

"I just want to teach these loudmouths a lesson. They think just because we have a girl on our team we're lightweights."

"We live on a moon, loyal Manfink. We are lightweights."

"Where are Leigh and Marsh?"

Chris squinted and scanned the main field. "Methinks I spy one hulking side of beef and one raven-haired beauty in yonder field. Let's check it out."

The two friends jogged across the commons and onto the large playing field. Marshall Farley stood six feet, three inches, and weighed close to two-hundred-thirty pounds, most of it muscle. Short, blond hair adorned his head, giving him a distinctly military look.

He waved at Chris and Manny and threw the football to Leigh Quintana, a tall brunette with dark skin and blue eyes. Unfortunately, she had turned to see who Marshall was waving at and did not see the ball flying in her direction. Marsh yelled her name, and she pivoted at the last second, still managing to catch the ball.

Manny whistled and applauded, while Chris sat down in a hurdler's stretch to begin stretching. Leigh threw the ball to Manny, who motioned for Marshall to go long. He threw a beautiful spiral but immediately regretted the action as a stab of pain shot through his shoulder. He grimaced and began massaging the muscle.

Chris bent low over his straight leg. "That shoulder still bothering you?"

"A little. I keep forgetting to warm it up."

"Don't. We're only out here 'cause of you."

Manny stuck out his lower lip. "They started it."

"Yeah, but you had to go flapping your gums about how good we are."

Leigh broke in. "I thought it was sweet that Manny stood up for me."

"Most of those guys are on the football team," Chris grumbled.

Manny grinned. "It's a time-honored tradition—men sacrificing themselves on the altar of chivalry. Besides, we have Marshall!"

Chris glanced at Marshall, who raised his eyebrows, looking—Chris decided—entirely too friendly. He stood up. "Try to look more ferocious, will ya, Marsh?"

Marshall's face turned into a scowl and he howled like a rampaging beast, charging right at Chris. The transformation was effective, for Chris found his legs frozen in terror. He could only stare helplessly as the roaring behemoth came hurtling his way. Too late, he turned to run. Marshall grabbed him around the middle and shook him like a rag doll, mercilessly.

Chris laughed and gasped for breath. "Okay . . . you win! . . . Save it . . . for . . . the game. . . ."

The group dissolved into laughter, and when the other team arrived, they were considerably more relaxed. They watched the other team warm up, trying not to feel intimidated by their superior speed and agility. All too soon it was time to set up the goal sensors and strap on the belts with the brightly colored flags.

This particular version of football had its origins in football and rugby, with a smattering of soccer thrown in for good measure. There were four players on a team, and the ball was shaped like a small watermelon, without seams or laces. At the start of the game, instead of a kickoff the ball was placed in the center of the field, with the team players alternating in a circle around it.

The captain of the visiting team was to call the ball into play, at which point the players tried to clear the ball from the circle with their feet. Then they could pick up the ball with their hands and run. Forward motion stopped when one of the flags was removed from the player with the ball.

With the sensors set up, the teams huddled on opposite sides of the field. Chris led off in a team prayer. "Lord, thanks for a chance to play today . . ."

Manny cut in ". . . please help us destroy these guys . . ." Leigh kicked him in the shin. "Ow!"

Chris continued. "Please help us play the best we can . . ."

". . . and help them look like idiots . . . Ow!" Manny said, receiving further correction from Leigh.

Marshall tried to pick up where Chris left off. "Please don't let anyone get hurt . . ."

". . . at least nobody on our team . . . Ow! Leigh! That hurts," Manny said, cradling his leg.

"Then stop praying like a jerk."

"Amen," Chris added, shrugging helplessly.

The teams arranged themselves around the ball, and Chris counted down from three. There was an eruption of frantic activity, as each player tried to kick the ball out of the circle.

Marshall maneuvered his foot under the ball but only kicked it into the chest of an opposing player, who caught it on his knee before looping it out and away in a high arc. The circle burst apart as both teams raced for the ball, each one ready to be on offense or defense at the moment of possession.

There was a free-for-all and the other team came up with the ball, setting up a beautiful open field pattern. Chris was almost on the guy with the ball, when his feet slipped, sending him sprawling. This allowed the other team, through a series of lateral passes, to score on the first play.

Chris lay sprawled on the field, glaring at Manny. "Thank you so much. I'm so glad to be playing these guys."

Manny shrugged and took the ball out of bounds for the inbound pass. He fired the ball in Marshall's direction, but an opposing player came from nowhere, snagged the ball with one hand, and ran it in for a goal.

The rest of the game continued in the same vein, with two notable exceptions. Halfway through, Leigh stole the ball from the other team and ran nearly the full length of the field, using a combination of sharp cuts and devastating fakes. When she blazed across the goal line, her teammates howled their appreciation as the other team grudgingly paid their respects.

Their only other score was on the last play of the game. They were set up for a sweep one yard from the goal, with Marshall at center and Chris at quarterback. On the snap, Chris charged up the middle. Marshall caught him, converting his forward motion upward, and threw him over the opposing team and across the goal line. They lost the game, but somehow it didn't matter anymore.

Both teams had shaken hands and were walking off the field when Chris noticed a new face on the sidelines. The fellow was just over six feet but very slender, with wavy sandy hair and thick glasses. A couple of guys on the other team saw him, too. Their eyes grew wider and they began whispering among themselves. One of them threw the ball at him and he caught it instinctively.

"Hey! Not bad. Nice catch, Doctor Alger." The other team continued on their way.

Dr. Alger tossed the ball in their direction and began walking toward Chris. "Are you Chris Graham?"

"Yeah, that's me."

"My name is Garrett Alger. I have a proposition for you, if you would care to meet me in the Student Union Building in half an hour."

Chris looked puzzled. "Sure."

Garrett nodded and walked away without another word. Chris's teammates joined him, curious.

"What was that all about?" Leigh asked.

"That was Garrett Alger. I've seen some amazing stuff about him in the *Scientific Journal*. I think he's here doing graduate work in artificial intelligence."

Manny was trying to place the name. "There was an article about him in the newsletter. Late twenties. Half dozen doctorates. He aced his entrance exams. Finished in fifteen minutes

12

and then asked the professors some questions they couldn't answer."

Marshall looked interested. "Impressive. What could he possibly want with the likes of you?"

Chris ignored the barb. "He said he has a proposition for me. Wants to meet me at the SUB in half an hour."

"You gonna go?" Leigh asked.

"Are you kidding? This guy has one of the finest scientific minds in the solar system. I'd be happy just to carry his books."

Curiosity clouded Manny's face for a moment. "If he's so smart, why is he still in school?"

Chris snorted in disgust. "Some people *enjoy* learning, mush-for-brains."

Manny glanced in Garrett's direction to make sure he was out of earshot. "Well, he's got the head for it. Look at the size of that thing."

Chris punched Manny in his bad shoulder. "Knock it off! Your head is too small for your body and we don't call you *Pinhead.*"

Leigh and Marshall were laughing. Manny rose up in mock indignation.

"No. You just call me *Scummy.*"

Chris smiled condescendingly. "Spare me your crocodile tears. You aren't the injured party here."

Manny rubbed his shoulder. "I'm not so sure. Bad enough we got slaughtered like we did."

Leigh and Marshall parted company with them, and Manny and Chris started for the showers, each favoring his own battle wound.

"Listen, next time you're talking to a professional football player, forget you know how to play the game," chided Chris.

"You're a fine one to talk, Butterfeet."

"I don't have to take this kind of abuse."

"Sure you do. You're the captain."

CHAPTER 2

The day was still bright and clear when Chris headed for the SUB, his mind awash with possibilities. Realizing there was no way to guess what Garrett's offer might be, he pushed both apprehension and wild dreams out of his head and said a quick prayer, trying—though not very successfully—to leave the whole thing in God's hands.

He walked in the front door of the SUB, passed the communications center, and turned left into the student lounge. Garrett was sitting in a booth along the far wall, writing in a small notebook. Even when Chris sat down across from him, he made no sign that he knew Chris was there. Chris chanced a peek at the notebook. The symbols were a total mystery.

Finally, Garrett stopped writing and looked up. "What do you know about artificial intelligence?"

Chris was taken aback by the lack of pleasantries but replied calmly, "I know that most of the things we use every day have integrated circuits designed to adapt to the user."

"Have you heard of Sentient Heuristics?"

"A little."

"*Sentient* simply means something is self-aware, and *heuristic* . . ."

". . . means it is capable of learning," Chris finished.

"Correct. Up until about eighty years ago, there was an entire branch of science dedicated to the creation of a sentient, heuristic computer."

"That sounds familiar. They were . . . Techno . . . Techno . . ."

"Techno-Humanists."

"Right! They wanted a utopia where machines did all the work."

"That's oversimplified, but basically correct. Actually, the technology had been around for decades, but using the only model available—the human brain—they were unable to duplicate the incredibly complex interconnections."

"Didn't they finally succeed?"

"Not exactly. Thiokol/Marrietta developed a molecular scanner, capable of mapping the unique patterns in a human brain. It's called *engrammatic mapping*. This meant they could make a blueprint of all the connections in a person's brain and duplicate it in the laboratory."

"I knew it was possible to map engrams, but I thought Thiokol/Marrietta was dissolved by the Stockman Antitrust legislation."

"That was later. The ability to replicate anyone's brain, with or without his consent, proved a terrifying prospect. When the societal implications were leaked to the media, a massive convocation of human rights groups issued a resolution calling for the cessation of work on all sentient machines. Sentient Heuristics became a volatile political subject and they lost their funding."

"And nobody has tried it since?"

"It's too dangerous. Any company associated with it runs the risk of economic sanctions."

"Why couldn't a scientist use his own brain for the blueprint?"

Garrett shook his head impatiently. "The prototype isn't the problem. Think how this technology could be abused, if it ever became generally available."

Visions of villains stealing people's brains flooded Chris's thoughts, and he frowned. "So, what's your proposition?"

"I have developed a prototype of a circuit that will allow me to create a brain without using any individual as a blueprint. I am putting together a team in an effort to assemble a synthetic organism."

"You mean an android?"

15

"I mean a synthetic organism. Completely original, capable of learning, self-aware, precisely based on homo sapiens. If we are successful, it will take a doctor to tell that the organism isn't human."

Garrett returned to his notebook and jotted down a few more symbols. Chris was lost in thought.

Garrett stopped writing and asked without looking up, "Are you interested?"

"Yes!" Chris blurted, wishing that he hadn't sounded so eager. He regained control of his voice with some effort. "It sounds like a fascinating project."

Garrett smiled blandly. "I think it will be. I'm delighted to have you on board. And please keep this in the strictest confidence."

"Whatever you say." Chris took a last look at the notebook. "Incidentally, what is that you're doing there?"

"I'm creating a new branch of mathematics. I call it *Subtemporal Irrelativity*. I'm hoping they'll accept it as my doctoral thesis."

Chris couldn't think of anything to say except "Wow," and that seemed idiotic, so he changed the subject. "When is our first meeting?"

Garrett stood up. "Thursday night at six-thirty in my lab on the second floor of Folsom Hall. Don't be late." He walked quickly out of the lounge, leaving Chris alone in the booth.

The young man gazed after him thoughtfully. "Don't worry. I won't be," he murmured.

Back on Earth, shortly after dawn Eastern Standard Time, Dr. Nathan Graham was sitting in his office in Fairfax, Virginia, studying an exceptions report. As head of forensics for SAFCOM, the largest communications company in the solar system, he had to wade through a lot of paper every day. When things were busy, he usually found himself doing a fair amount of detective work, but the slow times were the toughest, as they usually left him sitting in his office with nothing to do but sort papers. Realizing that he was daydreaming, Nathan tried to focus on the exceptions report in his hand.

Efficiency was down on the Mars generator and on the Io Converter Station. Both situations were attributable to recent solar flare activity. The note about the Io Converter Station made him think about Chris, and he wished there were a way to call him without spending a small fortune.

The last item on the report mentioned that replacement rings on the Misenberg Accelerator were nearly completed. Nathan's mind wandered for a moment, taking him back six months. During a trip to the Perimeter One space station at the edge of the solar system, his family had narrowly escaped disaster when the barge on which they were riding was pulled into the giant signal booster built by Joseph Misenberg. The last two rings had been destroyed by a fighter that flew into the accelerator to assist the barge. It had been a close shave for everyone.

He pushed the release button on his desktop and opened his desk drawer. Taking out a self-inking stamp, he labeled the report *Reviewed* and placed it in a slot at the top of his filing cabinet. "Weekly operations report," he said evenly, turning his attention to the next item on his "To Do" list.

The filing cabinet hummed for a moment and the report disappeared, whisked away to its proper slot. Nathan settled in for a long morning.

For Chris, Wednesday passed with excruciating slowness. At the Body Life meeting in the amphitheater, while his Christian friends and acquaintances were singing worship songs, he was trying to imagine what a living machine would be like. Later, instead of sharing and praying, he was wondering what it would be like to be written up in the *Scientific Journal*. At the end of the Bible study, he realized he hadn't heard a word.

Thursday was worse. He spent all morning thinking of ways an association with Garrett Alger could open doors after he graduated. Why, this could be the next big step in God's ongoing work in his life! So many things he could learn, so many people he could help.

Chris knew that good deeds without faith in the Lord were no good. But thinking was easier than praying, so he soon found himself thinking about God instead of talking to Him.

By lunchtime he knew his thoughts were getting out of control, but try as he might, he couldn't stop thinking about the project. Dreams and speculations kept interfering with his work. By midafternoon, halfway through his Engine Analysis and Repair lab, his partner was fed up with it.

Leigh took off her goggles and placed them on the table. "What's on your mind, Chris?"

Chris raised his eyebrows, trying to look convincing. "Nothing. Why?"

"You just messed up the same simple diagnostic for the third time."

Chris shook his head. "I'm sorry. I'm just distracted."

"It's this Garrett Alger thing, isn't it?"

"I promised not to talk about it."

Leigh could hardly contain her curiosity. "Can you speak in generalities?"

"I'm not sure I should."

"Don't you trust me?"

"No."

"What are you worried about? You asked me not to tell anyone about Shandra Harper, and I kept my mouth shut."

"Not so loud." Chris looked around to make sure no one had heard. "I told you, I was trying to open her door."

Leigh pressed her advantage. "Don't feel bad. I'm sure you're not the first person to smack someone in the nose on a first date. Happens all the time."

"All right, all right. Just shut up already, will ya?"

Leigh smiled warmly. "I'm just giving you a bad time. You don't have to tell me anything if you don't want to."

"It's not that I don't want to. . . ." He thought for a moment, and motioned for Leigh to move closer. "How much do you know about Garrett Alger?"

"Well, he's in one of my textbooks. I know they made a big fuss over him when he arrived."

"Suppose—hypothetically—that some brilliant researcher developed a new kind of circuit, a circuit that would lend itself to artificial intelligence applications, and he or she wanted to build. . . ." Chris hesitated.

"Build what?"

"A . . . living machine."

Leigh's mouth dropped open, but then she closed it quickly. "I would wonder—hypothetically—if they had lifted the ban on engrammatic mapping."

"Suppose he or she found a way to build the brain from scratch?"

This time it was Leigh's turn to look around to make sure no one was listening. "I'd think that was pretty incredible," she whispered.

"You see why a person would want to keep it quiet."

"Even if someone told me something so outlandish, I wouldn't breathe a word of it."

They set to work again on the rocket motor in front of them. Chris had the uneasy feeling that he had broken the spirit if not the letter of his agreement with Garrett, and now Leigh was distracted, too.

After a few minutes, Leigh broke the silence. "Do you suppose it would occur to this hypothetical researcher to consider the moral implications if he or she were successful?"

"Moral implications?"

"If someone creates a machine that is self-aware, does it have rights?"

"I don't know. I never thought about it."

"You probably should. As soon as your toaster can say 'I think, therefore I am,' it stops being an appliance and becomes. . . ." Her sentence was cut short by a firm hand placed on her shoulder. It was Professor Morisson.

"Miss Quintana, do you see that mark on the wall over there?" He indicated a six-inch indentation crisscrossed with burn marks and carbon scoring.

"Yes, sir, I do."

"Three years ago Marty Rosen was in my class. He liked to

chat with his lab partner and work at the same time until one day his assignment blasted off his workbench and created the impact crater you see on the far wall. The experience. . . ."

Chris snorted.

"Something funny, Mr. Graham?"

"Not at all, sir."

"I thought not. As I was saying, the experience was not without its exciting aspects, but I would dearly love to avoid a repeat performance. I would therefore appreciate a reduction of activity in your mandibular region, with a corresponding increase in your attention to the assignment."

With that, the professor moved on. Leigh glared at Chris, who was busily pretending to study the exhaust valves and biting his lip to keep from laughing.

When the afternoon finally ended and dinnertime rolled around, Chris found he didn't feel like eating anything. He killed time in his room until only a quarter hour was left, and then he jogged over to Folsom Hall. The second floor was dedicated to doctoral students; each lab customized to the specific needs of the user.

Chris found Garrett's lab without difficulty and pressed the call button. The door slid back soundlessly into the wall. Hesitantly he stepped across the threshold and surveyed the room. With a pang of disappointment, he realized he had been expecting a grand display of technological wizardry, not the pedestrian collection of machines stationed around the walls.

Besides the machines and adjacent workbenches, the only other furniture was a long, gray worktable in the center of the room surrounded by black plastic chairs. Coupled with the shiny drabness of the concrete floor, it made for very austere surroundings.

Garrett was sitting at a computer workstation along the righthand wall, energetically keying in data. He took no notice of Chris's entrance, except to say in a thick German accent, "Velcome to my laboratory, Igor. Please zit down."

Chris had not expected anything remotely humorous and

stared for a moment in surprise before finding a seat. Then he realized Garrett had been parodying Dr. Frankenstein and laughed out loud. Garrett smiled but continued inputting numbers. "Finally made the connection, did we?" he asked rhetorically.

As Garrett said nothing further, Chris made further inspection of the room and found that most of the machines were of a type he had never seen before. The door had closed as quietly as it had opened; a control panel with a video screen gave a view of the outside hallway, which explained how Garrett had known who was at the door.

The call signal sounded, and there were two more people on the video screen. Garrett looked up briefly from his workstation, pressing a button on the side of the workbench. The door slid open, and in walked a man in his early twenties wearing slacks and a white shirt, followed by a shorthaired girl who looked like a student, carelessly dressed in a gray sweatshirt and jeans.

Garrett asked the newcomers to join Chris at the table, promising he would be with them shortly. They sat down, exchanging shrugs and looks of bewilderment with each other. Garrett joined them a few minutes later but only stared at his hands until the others began to feel uncomfortable. Finally he spoke.

"Let me begin by saying that from this moment on, everything that goes on in here is strictly confidential. I'm afraid I'm not very good at interpersonal dynamics. I suppose we should go around the table and introduce ourselves. My name is Garrett Alger. I am a doctoral student in Artificial Intelligence and Mathematics, and I like pizza."

The other man at the table cleared his throat. "My name is Brian Melasco, associate teacher of Computer Sciences. You can call me Brian. Or Brain, if you're dyslexic. I am twenty-three years old and must confess a predilection for mint chocolate chip ice cream."

When the girl spoke, her voice was surprisingly warm and feminine, considering her tomboyish appearance. "I'm Cory Tabor, double major Bioelectrics and Chemistry. Fourth year with three semesters to go. My mom makes these incredible Angel Hair Tarts."

Chris couldn't help himself. "Angel Hair Tarts?"

"They're pastries, with unsweetened fruit filling and spun sugar on top."

"Sounds great. She hasn't sent you any recently?"

"Sorry."

Chris shrugged and addressed the group. "I'm Chris Graham, Engineering and Mechanics, and I don't know what the heck I'm doing here."

"Could you tell us a little about yourself?" Garrett prompted.

"Oh. Right. Umm. . . ." A silence ensued as he tried to think of something interesting, but he didn't really have a favorite food. Then it hit him. "I collect tiny transmitters from dead insects."

Cory snickered and Brian said, "That's something you don't hear every day."

For the first time in their brief acquaintance, Chris saw a look of interest on Garrett's face. "Excuse me?"

Brian tried to explain. "The insects grown by the entomology department are implanted with tiny transmitters that monitor life signs. It was the only way to keep a balance in the ecosystem."

Garrett looked amused. "I must have missed that."

Brian smiled kindly. "Perhaps you should get out more."

Garrett looked thoughtful. "Perhaps. But let's get to the subject at hand. You are all aware of my intention to build a synthetic organism. What I didn't tell you is how. You are each here because of your work. Brian, because of your postgraduate work in human psychology and computer programming; Cory, because of your innovations in bioelectrics and chemistry; Chris, because of your original approach to mechanical engineering and robotics."

Garrett leaned back in his chair, scrutinizing each face around the table. "Before we go any further, I have to ask if you're sure you want to participate. I cannot pay you for your work. Your only reward will be the thrill of making something completely new with a team of talented people. Brian?"

"After our initial discussion, I did a little checking. What you are proposing doesn't appear to violate any interstellar laws or Space Sciences Academy regulations," he smiled wryly, "though I suspect it may be because no one ever did it before. I will therefore participate on one condition. My association with the faculty must not become an issue. I'm here as a member of the team and nothing more."

"Agreed. Cory?"

"It's going to be tight with my studies, but I'll make it fit somehow."

"Chris?"

"Just one question. Have you considered the moral implications if we're successful?"

"If you are referring to the moral implications of creating a living machine, I have."

"And?"

"In my opinion it is the quality of sentience—*cogito, ergo sum*—'I think, therefore I am,' that is at least part of the foundation for all of our celebrated adherence to what we call *human rights*. If we are successful, the machine will not be human, but as a sentient lifeform it should still be treated appropriately."

"What would you think is appropriate?" Chris asked.

"To begin with, from the moment self-awareness is determined, I will do no further testing or modifications without the consent of the organism."

Chris nodded. "That sounds like a good start. Count me in."

"Excellent. Come with me please."

They followed him to the control panel by the door.

"I will need a thumbprint scan from each of you to provide access for you to the lab. It is important that you understand that by submitting to the scan you are entering into a nondisclosure agreement. If you reveal to anyone anything you hear, or see, or do in the lab, you may be subject to legal action."

They all nodded and Brian placed his right thumb on an oval pad set into the control panel. Light shone for several seconds under his thumb, as the words SCANNED and then VERIFIED appeared on a small monitor.

The light shut off and Garrett said, "That's it. Next."

Cory stepped up and put her left thumb on the pad.

"Right thumb, please," Garrett requested.

"But I'm lefthanded."

"Yes, but the outside access panel is on the right side of the door."

"Oh."

When Cory and Chris were finished, Garrett broke into a broad smile, relieved to have the formalities over with. "At last, my friends, we can eschew the veil of secrecy, for we are bound until death—or for three years, whichever comes first."

Despite some surprise at the sudden improvement in his demeanor, Chris and the others found themselves returning his smile. *Somewhere beneath Garrett's tremendous intellect, maybe there's a boy who still knows how to have fun,* thought Chris.

Garrett led them to a workbench with a plain black box on it. "With all due humility, I think you will find this fascinating."

The box was twelve inches square, with two buttons on the front.

"What's it made of?" Brian asked.

"My own version of obsidian. Almost no expansion or contraction with fluctuating temperatures. But I didn't bring you here to show you the box."

Garrett pushed one of the buttons, and a large hole appeared in the top. Tongues of vapor roiled up from inside the box and over the edges.

"What's in it?" Cory asked, peeking inside the blackness.

Garrett waved away some of the vapor and pressed the other button. "Watch."

From the hole slowly rose something shiny and deep azure blue. Whatever it was, it was beautiful.

Cory found her voice first. "It's . . . it looks like . . ."

Brian finished for her. "A brain. You've already built it?"

"I started six months ago."

Resting on its pedestal above the box, the two hemispheres were clearly visible, as well as the cerebellum and medulla oblongata. Between the hemispheres, Brian could even see the corpus callosum.

He stared at the brain like a man hypnotized. "How did you do it?"

"I worked with Lloyd Whitlock, the head of Doctoral Studies, to outline the scope of the project. With that done, all that was left was research, design, and construction."

Brian was amused by Garrett's audacity. "You can't believe how arrogant that sounds. You make it sound as if you were building a birdhouse."

"No arrogance intended, but if your plans are adequate, it is like building a birdhouse—assuming you have the right materials. The academy went to great lengths to get me here. So long as I am able to produce, I have written permission to use anything I deem necessary."

Cory was still staring at the brain. "I don't recognize this crystal formation. It looks a little like onyx. How did you build this thing?"

"You are all familiar with neural circuits?"

Cory smiled sheepishly. "It wouldn't hurt to hear it again."

Garrett put on his student teacher voice. "About forty years ago, LaRoan Wallis developed the first neural circuits, which stored and transmitted information much as the human brain does. As the circuits were refined, they greatly facilitated the creation of heuristic machines—machines capable of learning—which accounts for their proliferation in our current society."

Brian examined the brain again. "But those aren't neural circuits."

"The skeletal substructure is a series of neural circuits that attach all the parts to each other."

"But what is the rest of it? What's the cerebrum made of?"

"I used molecular etching techniques to lay down strips of gallium arsenide on the circuits. Then I modified a genetic replicator to produce some generic strands of DNA."

Brian looked alarmed. "Genetic replicators are only licensed to the Center for Congenital Disease in Phoenix."

"I have a friend on staff there. I only borrowed it for a few weeks and returned it in perfect working order."

"No doubt. What was the DNA for?"

"I had been fiddling around with gallium arsenide at the subatomic level and stumbled onto a way to make it grow in crystalline form."

Cory was incredulous. "That's not possible."

"I assure you, it is. But the growth of the crystals is stimulated by heat, and they have no lattices."

"Pure, crystalline gallium arsenide," Cory marveled. "You're going to be a very rich man."

Brian interrupted. "That still doesn't explain what you needed the DNA for."

"I isolated the sections responsible for development of each part of the brain, then used them as templates to program an army of nanites."

"Nanites! Do you have any idea how dangerous that is?"

"Dangerous?" Chris interjected. "They're just microscopic robots."

"At the risk of sounding condescending," Brian responded, "I have heard horror stories about malfunctioning nanites attacking their programmer's nervous system. And worse."

"Dear Brian, do you think me a fool?" Garrett asked patiently. "I took extraordinary care in programming my nanites. I sent them out in teams with knowledge of each other's instructions. Any deviation from the program by a single nanite would have resulted in its immediate destruction by the members of its team."

"But why nanites?"

"I couldn't figure out a way to impose the genetic code in the DNA directly on the crystals. So, I equipped the nanites with rubidium lasers and programmed them with the DNA as a roadmap. In thirty-seven hours, forty-one minutes they grew the brain you see before you. And incidentally, they were all accounted for when the job was done."

Brian was visibly relieved. "What about the actual neurons, axons, and all the rest?"

"That comes next."

Garrett pushed the button, lowering the brain back in its case, and the group gathered around the worktable again. He punched some commands into a keypad that Chris had mistaken for a calculator, and the tabletop, which clearly was no ordinary tabletop, displayed a schematic of the brain they had just been examining.

"Nice table," Chris murmured.

Garrett folded his hands in front of him. "I have created the brain. Brian, you will create the mind. We will work together and make liberal use of the data bases on the mainframe. Cory, you will help me finish all the connections in the brain, including all the connections to the body through the brain stem. Chris . . ."

"Let me guess. I'm going to be body building."

". . . you will assemble a chassis, humanoid in form, which will serve as the body. We can forego bodily functions other than standard mobility and dexterity."

"It would be a lot faster to use a standard android chassis."

Garrett shook his head. "The androids I have seen look like robots. Our finished product has to look like a man."

"If you want to pass this thing off as human, you'd better put in some bodily functions."

"Bodily functions are extraneous. Basic and intermediate motor function are of primary importance."

"A sentient being who can't enjoy pizza? You're a heartless brute, Doctor Alger."

Garrett smiled. "If we succeed, you can work on internal organs later."

The discussion continued on through the evening, and by the time they reached a good stopping place, it was well after midnight. As the project team, minus Garrett, walked out of Folsom Hall onto the cool grass, Chris realized he was much too excited to sleep.

"Anyone want to join me for a drink?"

Brian smiled weakly. "Thanks, but I don't feel as young as I look. My pillow beckons. I'll see you both tomorrow."

Cory shrugged. "Sure, I'll join you."

They walked across the field, enjoying the simulated moonlight, passed the athletic center, and headed to the Student Union Building. The SUB was closed, but next door was a twenty-four-hour student lounge called *The All-Nighter*. Midterms were still weeks away, so the place was nearly empty. They chose a booth near the door and ordered drinks by pressing buttons on the automated menu mounted on the wall. Chris finally broke the silence.

"Well, what do you think of our project?"

"It sounds . . . challenging. But I'm not sure it can be done."

Chris had his own doubts but only nodded. An awkward pause was interrupted by the arrival of the drinks, presented by a robot tray on wheels. They put their drinks on the table, and the robot waiter hummed quietly back to the kitchen.

Cory took a sip of her drink and began poking the ice with her straw. "What do you think of our project leader?"

Chris thought for a moment. "He's not what I expected."

"He gives me the creeps."

"Why do you say that?" Chris said, also taking a drink.

"His mind doesn't work the way ours do. I'm not sure he isn't crazy."

"I don't think he's crazy, but I know what you mean. It's hardly his fault, though. I mean, the guy graduated from high school when he was twelve and finished his undergraduate work summa cum laude in two years. He's got four doctorates and he's working on two more. Besides, he said himself—he's not good with people."

Cory sighed. "I just hope I'm not in over my head."

"We're all in over our heads. That's why it's going to be a blast."

CHAPTER 3

The executive conference room at Defense Concepts, International—located as it was on the top floor of one of the tallest buildings in Austin, Texas—was an impressive sight with the late morning sun streaming in the crystal clear windows that made up the east wall. A synthetic oak conference table (the wood was indistinguishable from the real thing) stretched the length of the room, surrounded by genuine leather seats. The table could seat seventy managers, fully loaded, but at the moment only twenty-one seats at the north end were occupied.

Morgan Henderson, President and Chief Executive Officer, was in the middle of his quarterly review with the department vice-presidents. As the executives gave the figures for their respective regions, Henderson sat back in his chair and grunted his approval. He was a short, stocky man, with a face that looked as if it had been chiseled from granite. That face now looked more unapproachable than ever. Margins were up, several large procurements were coming out over the next three months, and it looked like the stakeholder proceedings to have him removed were losing steam. So long as the company was performing the way it was, they were going to have a hard time convincing anyone they needed a change at the top.

Jerome Riggs, Vice-President of Middle East Operations, finished his presentation and sat down. Just as the next man was about to stand, Riggs raised his hand.

"Mr. Henderson, we're having a minor problem with the Egyptian Alliance. The latest skirmish with Israel has made the region very unstable. As you know, the Alliance and Israel are both valued customers. We have been approached by both sides with substantial orders for additional ordinance."

"What's the problem?"

"The Alliance is requesting enough neutron generators to wipe out the entire population from Gaza to Jerusalem. It is one of the most lucrative offers we have received in the past five years."

"You have done a cost-benefit analysis?" Henderson asked, his eyes narrowing slightly.

Riggs pulled a sheet out of his briefcase and handed it to Henderson. "Of course. The order from the Alliance would exceed the projected revenue from Israel for the next three years."

"That's a big pile of money, Mr. Riggs, but we must always keep the future in view. Giving one customer the means to annihilate another could seriously effect our five-year projections. Always remember, we must never give them what they need to wage total war. Police actions, incursions, even terrorist activities are acceptable, even desirable, but if one war machine knocks out the other, we lose a customer. Understood?"

"Clearly, sir."

The broad double doors opened abruptly and a tall, well-dressed, broad-shouldered man with closely cropped white hair stepped into the room. Henderson eyed the newcomer with distaste.

"Mr. Wagner, we are in session."

"I know. I'm afraid Mr. Smith has made an unscheduled visit."

"Gentlemen, you will excuse me."

Henderson was on his feet in an instant and headed toward the doors, careful not to touch Mr. Wagner as he passed. A short walk down the hall brought him to his office, a palatial construction of mahogany and crystal. His receptionist, Glynnas, was at her desk, already anticipating the situation.

"Mr. Smith is waiting for you in your office, Mr. Henderson."

"Thank you, Glynnas. Hold all my calls. I don't want any interruptions."

Henderson strode into his private office, closing and locking heavy double doors behind him. The room was spacious; one corner contained his massive desk, while various elegant collections of chairs and sofas provided the surroundings for different social requirements.

Sitting in a high-backed chair to the right was a man in uniform. He nodded slightly as the two men made eye contact but made no other move.

"Welcome, Mr. 'Smith.' I'm so sorry I was not available to receive you, but your visit was unexpected."

"This isn't a social call, Mr. Henderson. I just reviewed your project update. I want to know why we are a month behind schedule."

"These things take time, Mr. Smith. What you have requested has never been done before. We encountered some early setbacks, but we expect to make up the lost time in the latter phases of the project."

"Our response is due at the end of the next quarter. I am out on a limb here. If anyone finds out I am talking to you, I'm going to prison, and you will be barred from Department contracts for life."

"There are always risks associated with any high benefit enterprise. Risks can be mitigated." Henderson pulled a cigar out of a box on his desk but did not light it.

The haunted expression on Mr. Smith's face was almost pitiable. "Yes, but my risks are personal. I want more money."

"You agreed to one percent of three billion dollars. Certainly three million is enough to secure your future?"

"I want five percent."

Henderson fixed Mr. Smith with his steely gaze. He could see the man was scared. Source selection officials never seemed to have much stomach for felonious activities. This was the kind of man who would turn on you the moment things got too hot.

"Out of the question. However, I agree that the risk to you is personal. I am prepared to offer you an extra point-five percent to help compensate you for the risk involved. The total stands at one point five of projected contract value. I suggest you take it."

The man in the uniform knew there would be no negotiating. He looked down at the floor, unable to maintain eye contact, and nodded slowly. He tried to calm himself with the thought that if the deal went sour, he could always give Henderson to the feds. Without a word, he stood up and walked toward the door.

Henderson could guess his thoughts, and turned his back with contempt, walking toward his desk. "Make no mistake, *Mr. Smith.*" He said the name as if it were an epithet. "If you betray me, you are a dead man."

The man in uniform looked sharply at Henderson and hurried out the door.

The afternoon following the orientation meeting in Garrett's lab, Chris skipped his Form and Structure class and dropped in on the Metallurgy Department lab. He was on a first-name basis with the professor in charge and knew most of the lab students pretty well. The lab was used for fabricating anything from student projects to replacement parts for spacecraft, so many members of the student body had been through the lab at one time or another.

Formal discussions were breaking up as Chris walked in. He grabbed the two students he knew the best and hustled them toward the front of the workshop.

"Hey, Chris!" Jimbo Rourke had worked with Chris before and wasn't at all surprised to find himself in tow by the determined young engineering student. The other lab student was completely amazed.

"What are you doing?" demanded Katie Norsling.

"Relax, Kaynors. We have a date with Doctor Jadwin."

"A date? What are you talking about? We don't have any . . ."

Chris cut her off as he addressed the professor, who was still gathering his class materials at the worktable up front. "H'lo, George. How's business?"

"Chris! It's been weeks, hasn't it? What have you been up to?"

"Actually, I was wondering if you had a few minutes to discuss a proposition?"

Dr. George Jadwin stopped shuffling papers and sat back down in his chair. "I take it your proposition includes the services of Mr. Rourke and Miss Norsling?"

Chris looked a little sheepish. "We haven't really discussed it yet. I don't have a lot of time for the usual formalities. I am working on a special project for Garrett Alger, and I'm hoping I can interest you in giving me some help."

Dr. Jadwin put on his patient look. "What sort of project?"

"Well, that's the sticky part. I'm not allowed to discuss the particulars."

Katie started to interrupt. "You want us to work on a project without knowing what . . . ?"

Chris held up a hand. "I can guarantee you it isn't like anything you've ever done before."

Dr. Jadwin smiled a smile that said "How do you know what I've done?" but said nothing.

Jimbo looked interested. "What can you tell us?"

Chris chose his words carefully. "We would be designing a skeletal chassis for a . . . a humanoid mechanism. I want it to be able to do just about anything a real person can do."

Dr. Jadwin scratched his head. "I take it you mean an average person, with basic homo sapien motor skills."

"Yes."

Katie was skeptical. "The skills required for any activity would be utterly dependent on the motivational drivers. What is your control mechanism?"

"I can't say, but if you agree to work with me, you would be free to make your own conclusions based on my schematics."

Dr. Jadwin pursed his lips. "What you propose is intriguing, but I'm not entirely sanguine about embarking on a project of this magnitude without more information."

Chris thought for a moment. "Let me speak hypothetically with you for a moment. With a project of the scope I have outlined, what are the most likely possibilities for the end product?"

Jimbo grinned. "A crash dummy?"

"Cute, but no."

"I've seen your propulsion systems. You could use one."

Chris ignored the jab and looked at Katie, who hazarded a guess. "An android?"

"That's a better guess than Jimbo's. Doctor Jadwin?"

"I'm not very good at guessing games, I'm afraid. You used the word *humanoid* earlier. Perhaps something more than an android?"

Chris beamed with admiration and closed the subject. "Anyway, I think you begin to see some of the possibilities."

Dr. Jadwin clearly saw some of the possibilities, as evidenced by his brooding expression. He stroked his beard methodically for several moments, then turned suddenly and looked at Jimbo.

"Mr. Rourke, I want to assemble a team consisting of you, Miss Norsling, Mr. Owen, and Mr. Trent. Chris will function as project leader. In accordance with his wishes, we will keep this very quiet."

"Thanks, George. I can't tell you . . . ," Chris began, but Dr. Jadwin cut him off.

"I'm not finished yet. The project sounds challenging enough, and hence a worthy vehicle for extra credit, but I will accede to it on one condition."

"Name it."

"We have to see the finished product."

Chris grinned. "Agreed."

Katie raised a hand. "Did you say you were working with Garrett Alger?"

"Yes."

"What's he like?"

"Brilliant . . . a little shy. I've never met anyone like him."

Dr. Jadwin stood and placed a huge sheaf of notebooks in his briefcase. "I've a meeting to attend. You and your team may use these facilities after hours. If you need anything, please speak to me first."

Chris clapped Jimbo on the shoulder. "We'll meet day after tomorrow. I should have some preliminary schematics by then."

"Do you need any help?" Katie asked.

"Thanks, but I don't want to overload your schedule."

"Listen, it's no trouble. I need the extra credit."

"Count me in, too," added Jimbo.

"Thanks, guys. You won't regret it."

Late the following evening in Garrett's lab, Garrett and Brian sat side by side before a computer terminal. Stacks of printouts littered the workbench nearby, and both of them stared intently at the screen. A half-empty pot of cold coffee sat among the papers, but they had long passed the point of needing a stimulant to focus their attention.

Brian typed in several lines of code and leaned back. "Okay. That should complete the link to the language data base."

Garrett reviewed the lines Brian had just entered. "What about foreign language?"

"One miracle at a time, please."

Brian stood up and grabbed one of the printouts—three hundred pages worth—and moved to the worktable. After several minutes of paging through the listing, he stopped and waved a hand at the stacks of paper on the workbench.

"I think we're going to have a problem turning all this raw data into a dynamic, multidimensional data base. None of the entries are indexed in such a way that we can mandate a linking scheme. Unless, of course, you want me to write ten billion lines of code."

Garrett came over and sat down. "They have to be indexed. The data base we got the listing from is multidimensional."

"True. However, the structure we are imposing is totally different. We could load a fair portion of the mainframe into the brain, but we would simply have a duplicate of the mainframe. To make full use of the storage media, we need a new way of cataloging and storing the information."

Garrett shook his head. "No. Not a new way. We need to

find an analog to the same input methods humans use every day."

"Well, the program doesn't have eyes or ears, and those are the primary input channels to the human brain."

"What about Broca's revised map in the psychology data base?"

Brian pushed the printout aside and rubbed his eyes. "I thought about using that. The map breaks down types of information into categories and shows in what part of the brain such information is typically stored. But we still have a problem with indexing."

"And linking. We've simulated the brain physically, but the intricacies of memory are much more complex. I think we can program basic motor functions without too much difficulty, but the higher functions involving cognition and independent thought . . . I can't see how to get there from here in the amount of time we have."

Despite his fatigue, Brian smiled. "You eat new branches of mathematics for breakfast and you can't come up with an algorithm to mimic human thought? For shame."

Garrett missed the humor completely. "The brain is heuristic. It will learn, but without context, learning is futile. So much of memory is linked to images. . . ."

Brian snapped his fingers. "Images! That's it. We've been thinking of a conventional data base, which is completely inadequate for a human mind. If we want the mind to know what a dog is, we need a picture, preferably a moving one. Actually, we need several pictures. The problem then becomes how to link them."

"There are hundreds of hierarchial tree diagrams in the artificial intelligence data base. Using them as a reference, the mind would know that *dog* is related to *mammal* is related to *animal* and so forth. Even the cross links, like *animal* to *living,* should be in there. Do you think you can create an adequate bridge to the tree diagrams?"

"I think so. If we can get all the world knowledge of a freshman in college, we will at least have a basis for the more complicated cognitive functions. Which brings up another question: Do we want to program in memories of growing up, family, hometown, that sort of thing?"

Garrett frowned. "Did you believe in Santa Claus when you were little?"

"Did I . . . ? I suppose so. Why?" Brian asked, perplexed.

"When I was about five years old, for the first time in my life I beat my older brother in an argument. He responded by telling me there wasn't any Santa Claus. I knew he was wrong and told my mother to tell him so. She just looked at me, and I got this sick feeling in the pit of my stomach. If we program in memories of family, I think we're asking for trouble down the road. Better to be absolutely honest about his origin."

"His? Did you say *his*?" Brian was always intrigued by the human tendency to ascribe personhood to machines.

"Sorry. I have a tendency to anthropomorphize. I suppose that's why I'm trying to build a living machine. If we are successful, the appellation may be appropriate."

"You can call it whatever you like, but we have a long road ahead. Why don't you get some sleep? I have a couple of things I want to try before turning in for the night."

Garrett agreed and headed for the door, while Brian returned to the computer terminal and stretched one last time before settling into his programming posture. It was definitely going to be a long night.

The second meeting of Garrett's team was scheduled for two weeks after the first, in order to give Brian and Chris time to do the preliminary work on their pieces of the project. Chris was spending so much time in the metallurgy lab, his studies were starting to slip. He knew down deep that the project was becoming an obsession, but he pushed the thought aside. Quitting the team was the last thing he wanted to do.

Sitting in his room after dinner on the eve of the second meeting, Chris was reading a communication from his folks. Things seemed to be going well, but he had a faint sense of uneasiness. For Chris, his relationship with his parents exemplified much of what was good and moral in his life. Whenever his behavior wasn't on track, contact with his folks made him uncomfortable.

His conscience tried to tell him he had been neglecting his friends by spending all his free time in the lab, but he pushed the guilt aside. His time in the lab just now was a necessary evil. It wouldn't last forever. He had just finished reading the communication a second time when Manny walked in.

"Hi, Manny."

"Howdy, stranger. Note from home?"

"Yup."

"How is everyone?"

"Great, I guess. My brother placed second in a chess tournament, and my little sister has a lead in the school play."

"Nice."

An uncomfortable silence followed.

"I haven't seen much of you lately," Manny said finally, sitting down. "Spending most of your free time in Folsom, I take it?"

"Metallurgy lab. Our second meeting in Folsom is tonight."

Manny looked out the window. "You're not going to tell me what you're doing over there, are you?"

"You want to tell me what goes on in the bio lab?"

"You know I can't."

"Well, then I guess we're stuck."

Manny frowned slightly, "Are you coming with us tonight?"

"Where?"

"We're supposed to go and help out at the medical center."

Chris looked apologetic. "I can't. I just don't have time."

Manny pulled his Bible off the shelf and turned to the book of Matthew. "'Come, you blessed of My Father, for I was hungry and you gave Me food, naked and you clothed Me, sick . . .'" he paused for emphasis, "'. . . and you visited Me.'"

"Oh, knock it off. Jesus also said the poor would always be with us. We can help out whenever we want to."

"Yeah, but lately you don't want to very much."

"It's just for a little while. This project can't last forever."

"What about the game on Saturday?"

Chris put his face in his hands. "Oh, no! I completely forgot. I'm scheduled in the lab all day."

"Great. Just great. Like we're going to stand a chance with three players."

Neither friend could look the other in the eye.

Chris stood up. "Well, gotta go."

"See ya later," Manny growled, as Chris disappeared into the hallway. He threw his pillow across the room in frustration. "Much later."

As Chris walked away he resisted an urge to punch the wall. Working with Garrett was a great opportunity. You'd think his best friend would understand that. Maybe things would lighten up in a few weeks and he could make it up somehow. Besides, this promised to be an exciting evening.

He walked out the front of the dorm and over to the metallurgy lab for what he hoped would be the last time for a while. Katie was already there and greeted him with a wave of her hand, but she couldn't take her concentration off the machine in front of her. She was alone in the lab, since their work was nearly complete.

Chris stood beside her and ran his finger down the seams of the mold into which she had injected liquid metal the night before.

"This is the last set, right?"

"Yes. I put the mandible and phalanges on one plate. I don't know how the lower teeth will turn out. I had one or two fused molars on the upper plate when we did the skull, but all the bones of the hands should be within a few microns of your specifications."

"So long as the dental configuration provides an adequate framework for speech, I don't care if all the teeth have cavities."

Katie released the latches holding the two sides of the mold together and pressed the button to open the plates. Embedded in the right side of the mold were several neat rows of finger bones and a jawbone, all made of a heavy alloy with a dark bluish tint. Chris pulled out one of the finger bones and examined it closely.

"Very nice. If these were white, I wouldn't be able to tell them from the real thing."

"The skeleton will be much heavier and stronger than human bones. The trade-off is that these bones won't heal if they get broken. We'll save the molds, in case you have any accidents."

"I can't imagine an accident severe enough to cut through this stuff, but that's probably a good idea. Where's the rest of it?"

"Over there. I borrowed a carrying case from the music department."

Walking over to the case, Chris opened the latches and peered inside. Like some bizarre collection of bones from an alien Davy Jones's locker, the skeleton-to-be glinted dully up at him from the foam-lined case.

"When will the injection molded parts be ready?"

"Day after tomorrow."

"You're kidding? All those pieces?"

"The injection molding machine is linked to the mainframe computer. All I have to do is access one of the medical programs that describe the generic shape and thickness of the different muscle groups and subcutaneous flesh of the human body. The mathematical file descriptions are interchangeable."

"Beautiful work, Kaynors."

"Glad to do it. Once you have the pieces assembled, have Doctor Jadwin look it over so he can give me the grade I deserve."

"Will do. Would you please assemble the team at sixteen hundred hours three days from now. . . ."

"Assemble the team? But we'll be finished, won't we?"

". . . at the Student Union Building. I want to thank everybody for their hard work."

Katie placed the last of the skeletal pieces in the case, secured the latches, and helped Chris wheel it through the maze of machinery in the lab to the door. Once they reached the sidewalk, Chris straightened up and placed a hand on Katie's shoulder.

"Thank you so much. I owe you big."

40

"You owe me big." Katie smiled and walked back into the lab.

Chris checked his chronometer. He was late.

In Garrett's lab, the team had already finished a quick meeting and were hard at work. Brian and Garrett were putting the finishing touches on the program that would generate the mind for the brain, and Cory was trying to prototype some neural connections. She had been trying to create the connections for the better part of a week but kept running into trouble.

"No good," Cory said, shaking her head. "Your crystals are still stealing the charge."

Garrett rose from his seat beside Brian at the computer terminal, walked over to Cory's workbench, and looked over her shoulder. "Have you tried shielding?"

"The connections are too small."

The door to the lab opened, and Chris entered pushing the carrying case full of bones. "You will be happy to know," he said, opening the case and unloading the contents on a vacant workbench, "that the guys in the metallurgy shop are taking a real interest in this." He held up what was unmistakably a femur, looking down its length like a rifle inspection.

"Nice legs," Brian said with a wry smile.

"Chris? We'd like to borrow your intuition for a moment," Garrett said from Cory's workbench.

Chris set the leg down and walked over. "What's up?"

"We need material for Cory's connections that conducts electricity better than gallium arsenide crystals."

"I don't know of anything that conducts better than your crystals. We could try superconductors."

"I thought of that," Garrett replied, "but there's no way to maintain the low temperatures once they're in place."

Cory furrowed her brow. "We've been reading about some experiments using superheavy elements to boost conductivity."

Garrett shook his head. "We'd have trouble finding the source elements necessary to create the superheavy elements in sufficient quantities on campus."

41

Cory was determined. "We'll have to order them from Earth, then."

"That could take months."

"You have a better idea?"

Chris's face brightened. "What about Europa?"

A rare look of curiosity took over Garrett's face. "One of Jupiter's other moons? It's a big ball of ice. So what?"

"It may look like just a big ball of ice, but the core is warm enough that there's a liquid sea between the core and the crust."

"I know that. You expect to find source elements in the water?"

"Why don't we see what the survey says?"

Garrett sat down at the computer terminal, and his hands flew over the keyboard. He peered intently at the monitor for a few moments, then began to read. ". . . molybdenum, palladium, uranium. . . ." He broke into a wide grin, "Well done, Mr. Graham."

Chris beamed at the compliment. "Does your sphere of influence include academy spacecraft?"

Garrett raised an eyebrow. "What do you think?"

Brian gave Cory a look of resignation. "Looks like we're going to Europa."

CHAPTER 4

Across campus from Folsom Hall, at the top of a beautiful, wooded hill, set back in the trees, was a small brick building fifty feet square. In keeping with the sylvan theme of the landscape, it had been designed to look like a wellhouse for a large spring. What it actually contained was office space for the SAFCOM employees in charge of running the Io Converter Station.

Site manager Nelson Rolark sat at his desk, scrutinizing a column of numbers on his daily operations report, hoping to find a mistake. He was a broad-shouldered man with a bushy, brown mustache and a moderate stoutness about his middle.

He pursed his lips, put the report down, and punched a button on his desk. "Coslin?"

"Yes, Mr. Rolark."

"I have your DOR in front of me. If these numbers are accurate, we have a mechanical problem."

"I agree."

"Meet me in the control room in ten minutes."

"You got it."

Nelson walked out of his office and down a short hall to a large metal door with a simple hand scanner beside it. He placed his hand on the pad, and the door slid with exaggerated slowness into the wall.

He passed into the hallway beyond, and the door closed behind him. Here he was technically outside the dome, cut off

43

from the fabricated civilization just a few feet away. The double doors at the end of the hall led into the vast interior of the converter station. He turned right just before the end of the hallway and walked into the control room.

The room was laid out simply, with an operator's console in the middle and machines lined against the wall. Bob Coslin was waiting for Nelson. Wally Jensen, the console operator, motioned for them both to come over.

"Hey, Mr. Rolark," Wally said, not looking up.

"Jensen. What have we got?"

"I'm not sure. There are no bad circuits and the solar flares have died down, but we're still at sixty-five percent efficiency."

"Any leads?"

"Well, some of the diagnostics suffered abnormal termination at Access Panel Two."

Nelson frowned. "The programs crashed at AP Two? That's not normal, is it?"

"No."

"Let's check it out."

The three men left the control room through double doors for the converter chamber—a space big enough to drydock an antique Navy battleship. The layout was surprisingly similar to a hydroelectric project, with something akin to large penstocks down the right side, rows of generators the size of small houses, and walkways and gantries crossing the ceiling.

They wandered through the maze created by the generators and ancillary machinery and shortly found themselves standing before a primary logic conduit. The access panel was four feet high and three feet wide, with only scraps of adhesive where the name plate used to be. Some enterprising technician had taken a black marker and scrawled a sloppy 2 on the panel.

They opened it up and peered inside. The operator pulled a small tester out of his pocket and went to work. Suddenly he stopped.

"I don't believe it."

Nelson was straining to see. "What is it?"

"I found our problem. The circuits aren't burned out. They're gone."

"Your diagnostic should have picked it up."

"These have been patched to hide the theft. Nice job. It would have worked, too, but I've been making some custom modifications. These were patched to factory specs."

"Who could pull off something like this?"

"Me. Jensen. One or two professors and a handful of students."

"Can you fix it?"

"Sure. I stock most of the small stuff."

"Good. Let's keep this under wraps for now. I want a quiet investigation."

Nelson left the two men at the access panel and headed back to his office. Gritting his teeth, he walked inside and slammed the door.

"I'm gonna get the jerk who did this."

At his desk in a large office in the administration building, Dr. Lloyd Whitlock was reviewing a student's thesis on the influence of celestial phenomena on nebula emissions. His mind was far, far away when a knock at the door rudely snapped him back to his desk.

He sat up straight and put the paper down. "Come in."

Nelson Rolark walked in and closed the door. "You're Lloyd Whitlock, Director of Doctoral Studies?"

"That's what it says on the door."

"Nelson Rolark, Manager of Site Services for Io Converter Station. Do you have a minute to answer a couple of questions?"

"Of course."

"I'll get right to the point. Some of our circuits have turned up missing, and all the evidence points to theft. I'm not trying to point the finger, I just want to find out who did it."

"Surely you don't think I. . . ."

"No, of course not. But I was wondering if any of your students might have done it as a prank or something."

"I doubt it. Several are working on projects that might require

45

the kind of circuits you use, but they can be easily ordered from Earth."

"That's what I figured. Well, I'm stumped. Sorry to have bothered you."

"Not at all. Good day."

Nelson let himself out and closed the door. Dr. Whitlock picked up his communicator and dialed a five digit code.

"Mr. Henderson, please."

"May I tell him who's calling?"

"Doctor Whitlock."

Pause. "Henderson here."

"We have a problem."

Evening hung warm and cloudless over the sprawl of Washington, D.C. Were it not for the muggy weather and swarms of mosquitos, it would have been a beautiful night for a walk.

In the nearby suburbs Dr. Nathan Graham had decided to stay indoors. The family still sat at the dinner table, but the dishes had been cleared some time ago, replaced by a board game.

Amie was furiously haggling with Millie over a piece of property, while Ryan moved his game piece around the board. He landed on what he thought was a piece of unowned property.

"I'll buy it."

Nathan laughed with devilish glee. "Buy it? I own it!"

Ryan reached for his money. "I hate landing on Dad."

The merriment was interrupted by a beep from Nathan's communicator. He took it from his belt and pressed the answer button.

"Nathan Graham."

"Doctor Graham, this is Milo Breck, Vice-President for Converter Services. I'm sorry to bother you at home."

"What can I do for you, Mr. Breck?"

"Some circuits were stolen from the Io Converter Station. I wouldn't normally bother you with something so trivial, but they're afraid it may have been someone from the academy."

"Then they know who did it?"

"Not yet. As you know, our company is a major contributor to the capital funds drive each year, and there are a fair number of students who come from influential families. Frankly, I'm not sure how to handle this."

Nathan put his hand to his forehead. "I understand. May I put you on hold for a minute?"

"Certainly."

Nathan leaned back in his chair, rubbing his eyes. When he leaned forward again, he was looking intently at Millie.

"He's right about the sensitivity of this thing. I may have to go myself."

"You must be joking. Off to Jupiter? Just like that?"

"If this situation is handled wrong or the media gets hold of it, we could have a real mess on our hands. The only way to make sure is to go myself. And before you shout me down, let me say that it could work out well for all of us."

The whole family was ready to talk at once, but he held up his hand for silence. He pushed the hold button again.

"Sorry for the delay, Mr. Breck. I've given it some thought, and I think I better handle this myself."

The voice on the other end was obviously relieved. "Wonderful! It's your call, of course, but thank you, Doctor Graham."

Nathan terminated the connection, and the room exploded in noise as everyone tried to speak at once.

"Nathan, that's a long time to be away. . . ."

"Can I go, Dad?"

"Daddy, you can't go! My play opens in eight weeks. . . ."

Nathan held up his hand for silence again. "First of all, the trip shouldn't take more than six weeks. I must go. If this got out of hand, it could damage the academy, not to mention the company."

Millie shook her head. "I know, but it's awfully sudden."

"Listen, if I could take you all with me, I would. But Amie has her play, and if Amie stays, so does Mom. Ryan, on the other hand. . . ."

47

Ryan's eyebrows rose in anticipation, but Millie cut in. "There is no other hand. It's the middle of the school year."

"I'm not sure, but I think a trip to the academy would count toward his College and Careers credit."

"Nathan Graham, you are a sneak."

"Look at it this way. Ryan will get a chance to see the academy, I'll get my work done, and we'll both get a chance to see Chris."

There was a long pause. Millie shook her head. "Well, if you have to go. . . ."

Ryan clenched his fists in victory. "Yes!"

Nathan looked soberly at his son. "We'll talk to your teachers on Monday. I'm sure they'll have a lot of work for you to take along."

Ryan unclenched his fists. Nathan smiled sympathetically. "We can work out the details tomorrow." He looked down at the game board. "Now where were we? Ahhhh, yes. Ryan, I believe you owe me twenty-four dollars."

"I told you, the project is proceeding behind schedule, but it is proceeding."

Dr. Whitlock was trying to control his temper. "Garrett, you know how important this is. If we can't deliver on time, we might as well forget the whole thing."

"I'm doing the best I can. You want it to work, don't you?"

"If we miss the delivery date, it doesn't matter either way."

Garrett shifted uncomfortably in his seat. "I didn't come here to argue with you about the schedule, but while we're on the subject, I need a shuttle to Europa."

"Why do you need to go to Europa?"

Garrett took a deep breath. "I need source elements for the neural connections. Work cannot proceed without them."

Dr. Whitlock knew an order from Earth would take weeks. He didn't like being forced into a decision, especially by one of his students, but there appeared to be no alternative. As Garrett watched, he called the spaceport and arranged for Garrett to be given a shuttle for a trip to Europa.

"Thanks, Lloyd."

"Just be sure you get back on schedule."

Garrett could hear the tension in Dr. Whitlock's voice, and thought it best to leave without saying anything more. Maybe they would be able to pick up some time during assembly and testing.

All Chris received in the way of preflight information was an abrupt call from Garrett telling him to be at Launch Bay Number 2 at 1600 hours. He was impressed by the level of respect Garrett seemed to command at the academy. *Yep,* he thought, *being on this team is definitely a good career move.*

For the moment, however, the issue was that he not miss the trip altogether. He was busily rummaging through his closet when there was a knock at the door. He kicked enough clothing out of the way to answer it.

There stood Leigh and Manny. Manny wasn't outraged, but his tone was more than indignant. "What's this we hear about you going to Europa?"

Chris had hoped to avoid such a confrontation. "News travels fast around here."

"And how long is this little excursion going to take?" Leigh asked, trying to hide her concern.

"Not more than a week, I hope," Chris answered, stuffing his last clean shirt into a duffel bag.

"You'll miss your classes."

"I'll just have to get caught up when I get back."

Manny looked at his friend in earnest. "This isn't just a trip to the zoo, you know."

"Relax. We'll have a professor along and a pilot who knows what he's doing." Chris grabbed his roommate's collar and looked at him with mock feeling. "Thanks for caring."

Manny threw Chris into a quick headlock and mussed his hair. "It's your neck. Just watch yourself out there."

Chris slung his bag over his shoulder and made for the door.

"Hey, we'll be hurtling through the cold vacuum of space, in a ship with over one hundred thousand parts, any of which could fail without warning, with nothing between us and oblivion but six inches of insulation and metal. What could possibly go wrong?"

The three friends left the dorm and headed east across campus for the wooded hill a half mile away. The illusion of sunset was being played out over the hills behind them, casting lovely red and orange hues on the fields around them.

Chris pointed to the top of the hill. "Have you ever watched the sunset from up there?"

Leigh shook her head, and Manny thought for a moment. "I don't think I've been up there at all."

"It's beautiful."

"What were you doing up there?"

"When I was first here, I took a tour of the converter station."

"I've been meaning to do that."

"You should. There's a lot of cool stuff up there."

They walked on in silence, enjoying the evening breeze, oblivious to the large vents in the hillside that created the artificial environment. When they came to the foot of the hill, they turned left and walked down a stone path, through a gravelly wash to the spaceport.

The entrance did not look like a launch facility. There were no doors, only a hole in the wall forty feet wide and eight feet high. The main receiving area was relatively spartan, with white speckled tile in the floor and a mosaic of tiles, three different shades of blue, on the walls.

A few chairs, sofas, and potted plants dotted the area, but the only place for transacting business was the counter at the far left end. Beside the counter was a huge, hermetically sealed door flanked by an armed guard.

Chris stopped to thank his friends for the escort. Manny reminded him that the Festival of Storms was only two weeks away. The day-long event took place once a year, when the hottest programmers on campus took a shot at the computer responsible for the weather patterns in the dome. The entire campus spread out on the hills and fields to view incredible pyrotechnic displays of lightning and astonishing meteorological effects prepared for the competition. Last year, Chris's entry had taken third place.

Chris assured his friends that he would be back well before the festival, though he doubted he would have time to participate this year. They exchanged hugs and Leigh kissed him on the cheek, then reluctantly his friends turned and left. Chris checked in at the counter and walked through the big door into the hallway beyond.

Launch Bay Number 2 was cavernous, eighty feet square and forty feet high with an arched ceiling, and outfitted with the usual collection of maintenance equipment, refueling apparatus, and spare parts. Two technicians were busy with the preflight check and didn't even notice as Chris walked by.

The shuttle was forty feet long and thirty feet wide, and something about it made him uneasy. He was examining it from stem to stern, inspecting all eight landing struts, when the thought hit him: *This looks like a giant beetle.*

Chris found the access ramp and walked into the shuttle. There was not much headroom, but at least he didn't have to bend over to enter. Marshall would not have been so lucky. He had entered amidships, so there were four cabins aft of his position, not including the engine room, and two half rooms forward, not including the cockpit. He turned right and peeked into the first room he came to. Cory was sitting on the bed putting drops in her eyes.

"Hi, Cory."

"Chris! We were beginning to wonder."

"Where are Brian and Garrett?"

"They're forward securing the last of the equipment."

"Which room is mine?"

"Just keep walking. You can't miss it."

He was at the end of the hallway before he found an unoccupied room. His room was as big as the others, but it still looked very cramped. A narrow bed took up most of one wall. There were a few cupboards, a tiny sink barely deep enough to wash his hands, and a small chair in the corner.

He threw his gear under the bed, then headed down the narrow hall in search of Brian and Garrett. A brief search brought him to the half rooms just aft of the cockpit. Ordinarily these would be used as a galley and utility closet, but the fixtures in both rooms had been removed to make more room for equipment and food stores. Brian and Garrett were in the room to the left, securing what looked like an old auto transmission.

Chris leaned in the door. "Permission to come aboard."

Both men looked up, and Brian smiled. Garrett looked down again and secured a loose strap. "Permission granted. Your timing is perfect. We just finished."

"What is that thing, anyway?"

"A geoseismic scanner so we know where to put down. We want a place where the ice is thin, but not too thin." Garrett stood up. "We have enough food for three weeks."

It occurred to Chris that all the living quarters were either spoken for or filled with provisions. "Where is the pilot going to sleep?"

Brian was headed out the door. "In Cory's room."

Chris did not like the sound of that. The three of them filed into the cockpit and found Cory sitting in the command seat.

Chris's eyes nearly popped out of his head. "You're the pilot?"

Cory smiled. "No need to panic. I learned to fly this thing when I was a freshman."

Chris wasn't convinced. "But you . . . that is . . . I thought one of the spaceport pilots. . . ."

Brian took the copilot's seat. "She's logged twelve hundred hours in the command chair, including a couple of field trips to Ganymede and Callisto."

Chris closed his mouth and strapped in behind Cory. "My apologies. What was Ganymede like?"

"Dirty," Cory replied, "but the view was incredible. You've been to the academy observation lounges?" All three of her teammates nodded their heads. "It's not the same."

Garrett strapped himself in behind Brian. "Please proceed with the preflight check."

Cory finished configuring the controls for takeoff and pushed a button on the console, causing the access ramp to withdraw into the shuttle and the door to be closed and sealed. She doublechecked the controls and thumbed the communicator.

"This is Harrier Shuttle in Launch Bay Number Two requesting permission to launch."

"Roger, Harrier. This is spaceport control. Atmospheric doors are secure. We are depressurizing the launch bay."

The lights in the launch bay went out, leaving only the landing lights and the launch pad illuminated on the outside. Inside the cockpit it was eerily quiet. Brightly colored lights from the instrument panel cast a distorted glow over the four passengers' faces.

The controller's voice came over the speaker. "Pressure to zero. Opening bay doors."

Without a sound, the arched ceiling overhead split and each half rotated down into the walls, revealing the pitch blackness of space. The carpet of stars was marvelous; the pinpoints of light too numerous to count. Even so, the opening did not look very wide. Years ago, when the spaceport was first commissioned, several shuttles had received minor damage during takeoff. The pilots soon discovered that by tilting the ship during takeoff, they could compensate and maneuver through the narrow opening.

"Launch bay doors are in position and secure. Harrier Shuttle, clear to launch."

Cory adjusted her harness. "Nice to know someone still knows how to open a door for a lady. I'm outta here."

"Roger, Harrier. Keep your nose clean."

Cory smiled and nodded, starting the engines and engaging the vertical thrusters. The shuttle shuddered almost imperceptibly and started to rise. She adjusted the controls, looking intently out the window.

Garrett turned in his seat so he could see better out the front. "Pitch to fifteen degrees."

Cory didn't want to take her eyes off the wall of the launch bay. "Brian, could you read it for me?"

Brian scanned the gauges. "Three degrees positive pitch . . . ten degrees . . . fifteen. Steady at fifteen degrees positive pitch."

Chris muttered a quick prayer under his breath as the shuttle rose through the opening and cleared the launch bay, passing between the doors without a scratch. The vast dome of the academy gradually dropped away beneath them, and Cory turned the ship around.

There was Jupiter. Monstrous, ominous, majestic—nearly filling the sky with its roiling maelstrom of orange, red, and gray. They had all seen the planet many times before, but no feeling person could fail to be awestruck anew by its gargantuan, foreboding beauty.

The comm speaker crackled. "Harrier Shuttle, you are free and clear to navigate."

Cory's attention snapped back to the business at hand. "Roger, control. This is Harrier Shuttle, off out."

Brian tore himself from the view and checked his instruments again. "I'm receiving telemetry."

The computer on board the shuttle quickly assimilated the navigational data transmitted from spaceport control, and Cory engaged the autopilot. The forward thrusters engaged, and the shuttle swept upward in a long arc over Io's angry surface. Chris watched a river of lava erupt from a small volcano, reminding him again why there were few field trips outside the dome.

He looked forward again, hoping that with the ship on autopilot, Cory might answer a few questions. "How long will the trip take?"

"Barring something unforeseen, we're looking at about three hours."

"How much of that will be on autopilot?"

"Most of it." She patted a small box beside her. "This little baby will do everything but land the ship."

Garrett leaned forward, addressing his question between the front seats. "Incidentally, why do they call this *Harrier?*"

Brian responded. "The Harrier was an old VTOL aircraft—

vertical takeoff and landing—used by the British Airforce and the U.S. Marines. The wings would rotate so the plane could take off straight up. They called them *jump jets.*"

Chris was amused. "Jump jets?"

"Since they required no landing strip, they were quite adept at 'hopping' from place to place."

Garrett leaned back in his seat. "Well, someone on the shuttle design team had a sense of humor. This thing looks more like a Japanese beetle."

Brian laughed. "Be glad they had some imagination. It could have been worse."

Cory snickered. "Control, the Bug is ready to fly. Roger, Bug. Keep your proboscis clean."

Garrett closed his eyes, with just a hint of a smile at the corners of his mouth. "You're right. It could have been worse."

Sunset over Austin, Texas, was often a beautiful sight, especially from the president's office at Defense Concepts, International, but on this particular evening Morgan Henderson was in no mood for appreciating beauty. He sat brooding behind the disorganized landscape of his desk, thinking about the only time in his life a project had come off without a hitch. It was one of the first contracts he had ever landed—a dozen all-terrain vehicles for the Army—and everything had gone exactly as planned. That had been almost twenty years ago, and every few weeks he wondered why nothing now ever went as smoothly as that project. The answer he always gave himself was the same: The universe was against him.

He watched sourly as the last sliver of the sun disappeared beyond the horizon, and then he viciously punched a button under his desk. A few moments later, a door opened and Lash Wagner walked in.

"Yes?"

"Mr. Wagner, please book passage for us to the Space Sciences Academy on Io. We will be staying for one week."

"Do you think that's wise?"

"If I didn't think it was wise, I wouldn't do it, you imbecile.

I don't like projects running behind schedule, and I don't think Whitlock is able to provide the necessary motivation. That's why I'm taking you along."

Lash Wagner smiled unpleasantly at the thought of torturing some helpless academy vermin. "When do you want to leave?"

"As soon as possible. This is one contract we have to win."

CHAPTER 5

Cruising at sixty thousand feet, the Air Australia transport *Silverwind* shot across the sky on a vector for its home base near Sydney. The seats in the passenger compartment were arranged four abreast, with two seats on either side of the aisle. On the right side, just behind the wing, Nathan Graham sat in the aisle seat beside Ryan.

Nathan finished off the complimentary soda provided a few minutes earlier and faced Ryan. "Now, you're sure you've got everything?"

"Dad, you checked my bag ten times before we left. Besides, it's not like we're going back for anything."

"True enough. Did your teachers give you any trouble?"

"It depends on your definition. They gave me plenty of makeup work."

Nathan laughed and ruffled Ryan's hair. "You'll do fine. This is going to be great."

After the transport had landed and taxied to its gate, Nathan and Ryan quickly located and boarded the ground shuttle to the launch terminal, arriving with only ten minutes to spare. They sprinted to the check-in counter inside, and Ryan had his first opportunity to check out their ship from the viewing window while Nathan presented their reservation vouchers.

The light cruiser they were going to be on for the next ten days stood two hundred fifty feet high, adorned with six large booster rockets. This would be Ryan's first vertical launch. All his other off-planet excursions had begun with a shuttle launched horizontally from the back of a high-flying aircraft to connect with an orbiting launch station. Nathan had asked for an opening on such a flight, but this was the only ship available on short notice.

He joined Ryan at the window with the vouchers. "We're all set."

Ryan nodded but didn't move. Nathan followed his son's gaze. "Feeling a little nervous?"

"Not at all. Just enjoying the view."

"That's good, 'cause there's not going to be much to see for the next couple of weeks."

Just then, the gate attendant's voice came over the intercom. "We are now beginning general boarding for Flight 208 to Io, Neptune, and the Perimeter One Station. Please have your tickets ready when you reach the gate."

When their section was called, they passed through the gate and followed a walkway to the elevator. Fifty feet up, after a couple of stops, it was their turn. They crossed a short, open walkway and stepped through a hatch into their reserved cabin.

Ryan pulled up short, astonished. The entire room was on its side. Their quarters were nothing fancy—a couple of beds, an assortment of storage compartments, and a tiny bathroom barely big enough for one—but the sensation was bizarre with everything secured for launch.

Nathan nudged him forward. "Everything will be right side up once we're in space."

After stowing their bags, they sat down in a pair of launch seats, mounted on what would soon be the wall, and strapped themselves in. A flight attendant stuck his head through the hatch to see how they were doing.

Nathan smiled disarmingly. "We've done this before."

The attendant disappeared. Ryan muttered, "Speak for yourself," but Nathan was too busy with the straps to take notice. The hatch was closed from the outside, and a panel slid down to hide the hatch. Without warning, the platform they were sitting on rotated until they were lying on their backs.

After several minutes, the captain's voice came over the speaker. "Good afternoon. This is Captain Steffans. I have a green light up here. Looks like we're all ready to go. Unfortunately, our launch window isn't for another ten minutes. Anyone not going to Io, Neptune, or the Perimeter One Station better get off."

Ryan started to feel nervous. "Tell me again why we're doing this."

"I have to investigate a theft at the converter station. You're going to check out the Space Sciences Academy. And I hope we both get a chance to see Chris."

"What's it like, launching like this?"

"Like having an elephant sit on your chest."

"Oh, great."

"Actually, it's not that bad. Remember when we took off in the *Silverwind* this morning, how it pushed you back in your seat? It feels like that, only more so."

Looking around at the simple accommodations, Ryan figured he would be stir-crazy in about three days. He settled back in his seat and consoled himself with the thought that most of his friends were in class about now.

"Liftoff in T-minus one minute."

Dr. Graham closed his eyes and offered a short prayer, as was his custom prior to every flight. Every three or four years, a passenger ship went up in flames. Three years ago it had been the *Pacifica*. One of her boosters tore loose during liftoff, and she crashed to the ground and exploded, turning the launchpad into a fireball. He could still remember the sick feeling of horror as he watched the videotaped footage again and again on the news.

As the captain began the final countdown, Nathan was comforted by the familiar words that came to mind: "Trust in the LORD with all your heart, and lean not on your own understanding." With some effort, he put his worry away and tried to think of happier things.

The launch was flawless. As the ship rose along its planned trajectory, Ryan decided his dad's analogy of an elephant on his chest was a good one. For several uncomfortable minutes, they both felt as if they weighed a thousand pounds; then, they were in space. The main engines fired for a half hour, then all was quiet and they were free to move about the ship.

The next hour was spent arranging their belongings and getting reacquainted with weightlessness. Pairs of specially treated shoes kept their feet on the carpet so they could walk. With the room in order, Ryan was ready to explore the ship.

"Mind if I take a look around?"

"Not at all. Oh! I completely forgot." He pulled a brochure out of his briefcase and handed it to Ryan. "I ordered some promotional materials from the Admissions Department in Cincinnati."

Ryan had heard Chris describe the academy, but he had never seen pictures. He opened it up and immediately understood why his brother liked it there. The fields. The trees. The pretty girls. Looking at the brochure, he had to admit he missed his brother. But at a place like the academy, he figured his brother probably didn't miss him very much.

The Harrier Shuttle completed its 160-degree arc around Jupiter at two hours, fifty-three minutes, assuming a low orbit around Europa. Brian and Garrett hauled the geoseismic scanner into the cockpit. Chris eyed it with some curiosity.

"Is it right side up?"

"No. It's on its side, actually," Brian replied. "This shuttle was not designed with heavy equipment in mind."

They hooked the machine up to the sensor array with a tangle of cables and switched it on. Not far below, the icy plains of Europa rolled by. Long, dark lines were visible in the ice, and the dearth of craters bespoke a surface much younger than its lunar counterparts. Brian fiddled with the scanner controls and began searching the monitor for a thin spot in the ice.

After a few moments, he looked at Garrett. "How much hose do we have?"

"Five thousand feet."

"I hope it's enough."

They searched for twenty minutes before Brian stood upright and rubbed his eyes. "I'm not getting anything thinner than ten thousand meters."

Garrett repositioned his glasses. "That's not good. We need a place where the water's warmer."

Chris nodded. "We could check for thermals."

Brian reconfigured the scanner for infrared. "Everyone strap in. Cory, give me some altitude."

Cory pulled back on the controls and the ship rose sharply. "Z-plus ten thousand meters."

"Anything?" Garrett asked, looking over Brian's shoulder.

"No . . . wait a minute. Looks like thermal activity at forty kilometers. Your new heading is two-seven-zero."

Brian reset the scanner, while Cory increased speed and brought the shuttle down in a steep parabolic arc along the new heading.

Chris felt nauseated. "Can we go back and pick up my stomach later?"

"Sorry," Cory said shortly.

Brian was watching the scanner and nodding. "Getting better . . . ten thousand . . . eight thousand . . . sixty-five hundred, reduce speed, please. Take us down to seventy meters."

Cory throttled back and shed the necessary altitude in a few seconds. Chris was glad he hadn't eaten lunch.

Brian kept monitoring. "Giving readings in feet. Forty-eight hundred . . . forty-three hundred . . . thirty-nine, that's our spot. New heading two-five-eight, one hundred forty meters from my mark . . . and . . . *mark.*"

Cory brought the shuttle in low, realized she was going to overshoot the mark by several yards, and cut the engines. The ship dropped a few feet and landed hard, throwing everyone against their restraining straps. Brian thumped the monitor. "Bull's-eye. Nice flying, Captain Tabor."

"We aim to please. Sorry about the landing." She turned to face Chris. "You ever been on a shuttle like this before?" He shook his head. "Stand at the door and watch."

Though puzzled by her instructions, Chris stood to one side

of the door and looked aft, while Cory flipped some switches on a box mounted on her left. To his amazement, the floor behind the cockpit began dropping away as the walls receded into the ceiling.

"Oh, this is drastically cool," Chris murmured.

The transformation took just under a minute, and when it was complete, they were looking down on an oval room thirty feet long and twelve feet high. The individual living areas were still discernable from outlines on the floor, but the only walls that remained were around the lavatory and the engine room in the back.

Chris walked down the newly formed flight of steps, followed by Garrett and Brian. Cory stayed behind to shut down all nonessential systems. As he reached the bottom of the steps, Chris stretched his arms out wide, luxuriating in the spacious feeling of the room.

"This is most drastically cool!" was all he could say.

"You haven't seen the best part yet," Brian said, walking over to a storage compartment and producing a key shaped like a tuning fork. "Garrett, would you like to do the honors?"

Garrett dismissed the offer with a wave of his hand. "Be my guest."

While Cory made her way down from the cockpit, Brian moved to the center of the room and got down on his hands and knees. Only by bending over could they see the faint outline of a panel in the floor. In each of the four corners was a circle an inch wide with two square holes corresponding to the key he held in his hand. He gave each lock a quarter twist to the left and the panel rose up from the floor a half inch.

They moved the panel aside, revealing a control panel underneath. Cory checked the gauges concurrently with Brian, pushed a button, and then examined the gauges once more.

"Steady at point four negative pressure," she observed. "There's the green light."

Brian nodded. "Let's open her up."

They grabbed the four heavy clamp latches and lifted the instrument panel out. There came a gentle hiss of escaping air, and Brian stood out of the way so Chris could see down the hole. It looked like a box full of ice.

Garrett couldn't resist taunting, "It looks like an icebox, but where's the beer?"

Chris shook his head, mildly amused but still puzzled. "That's not an icebox. . . ." His voice trailed off as he realized he was looking at the moon's surface.

Brian smiled with a hint of mischief in his eye. "Welcome to Europa, Mr. Graham."

"I wouldn't do that if I were you."

Nathan took his hand off his remaining bishop. "And what would you do?"

"If you move your bishop, I'll have your rook in two moves," Ryan said simply.

Father and son had returned from their tour of the ship, which hadn't taken very long. Besides the passenger cabins, the only facilities were a lounge not much bigger than their room, three food dispensers, and a tiny weight room which was already booked for the entire journey. The wide central hallway had reminded Nathan of the passenger section of a cruise ship.

Nathan moved his rook instead, putting Ryan's queen in jeopardy. "Check."

Ryan ignored the rook and moved a bishop from one corner of the board to the other. Nathan's king was trapped. Ryan's other bishop and a knight had all escape routes blocked.

"Checkmate."

Nathan laid his king on its side. "Thanks for the game."

Ryan sighed. "There's not much to do here."

"I think it looks like an ocean liner."

"Yeah. Without the ocean and without the liner."

Ryan sat down on his bed. He was already bored. "Can I watch some videos?"

Nathan sat down in a chair and picked up a book. "Why don't you get started on your school work?"

Ryan recoiled at the idea. *Gak!* he thought. *We've only just left. Of course, if I don't get it done, he'll nag me all the way to Jupiter.* Besides, there wasn't much else to do, and he hated having it hanging over his head. He looked wistfully at the video screen. "That's it. I'll do all my school work first and then watch videos till my eyes ache."

With the equipment set up and ready to go, the aft compartment of the Harrier felt much less spacious. The plan was to drill a hole through the ice and pump water from below into a distillation unit, then pump the waste water back down the hole. This would be accomplished through a double-lined hose that allowed liquid to pass up the center at the same time that liquid was pumped down through the outside layers. The distillation process could accommodate six hundred gallons of liquid an hour, producing three pounds of element-rich sludge.

The earliest field trips to Europa had suffered minor mishaps due to careless researchers and a lack of procedures. Before someone got hurt—or serious environmental damage could be done—the board of governors for the academy, in conjunction with the Global Department of Commerce, had been quick to institute rigid regulations regarding the taking of samples and similar activities.

It had taken the better part of a day to organize the procedure. More floor panels had been removed, exposing the distillation unit. Two metal frames had been assembled, one to hold the spool with the coil of hose, the other to feed the hose down the hole. There was a winch for the spool, and several environmental devices to monitor poison gases and other hazards. The drill was mounted on a six-foot rod at the front of the hose. If all went well, it would be like threading a very large needle.

Chris picked up the rod and examined the hose. "It doesn't look very strong."

"You'd need a pair of hydraulic bolt cutters to get through it," Brian replied, helping Garrett with the last of the monitoring equipment.

"How long will it take to get through the ice?" Cory wanted to know.

Brian set his chronometer. "At one hundred fifty feet per hour, twenty-six hours."

Garrett and Chris grabbed the rod and started drilling.

Brian looked uneasy. "You're sure we're authorized to do this?"

Garrett shot him an irritated look, "Of course. This is a heck of a time to bring it up."

"Sorry. I just don't want to be reprimanded by the board."

"Dr. Whitlock signed the papers himself."

Something about Garrett's tone of voice put Chris on edge. He sounded as if he were lying. If that were the case, Chris should say something—right now. If he were wrong, at best he would look a fool; at worst he would be dropped from the team. He tried to shrug off the uneasiness he felt, telling himself that he was imagining things. But his conscience had quietly begun to nag him.

Once the rod had disappeared and the hose was moving down the hole, it was just a matter of waiting. Garrett pulled out a notepad, sat on his bed, and started writing. Cory found a deck of cards with some chips and roped the other two into a game of poker.

"Why do pilots always want to play poker?" Chris asked.

"We like the risk. Straight five card draw."

Cory dealt the hand and they picked up their cards. They were busily sorting when Brian posed a question. "Do you believe in God, Mr. Graham?" He hadn't looked up.

Chris blushed, surprised by the abruptness of the question, but answered with confidence. "Yes, I do. Why do you ask?"

"I overheard you praying when we took off."

"Do you? Believe in God, I mean."

"I was raised a Catholic, so officially I suppose I do. But I haven't been to Mass in years. How about you, Cory?"

"My mom told me never to discuss religion with friends. It's your bet."

Brian glanced at his cards. "I'll pass for now. We're all thinking people here. Surely our relationships can withstand a little spirited discussion?"

"I'm telling you, it's a bad idea. Chris, it's your bet."

Chris was already more interested in the conversation than the game, but threw in a blue chip anyway. "Ten. I agree with Brian. Garrett, what do you think?"

Garrett stopped writing and looked up. "About what?"

"Religion as a topic for discussion."

"I'll save you the trouble. God does not exist." He returned to his notes.

Chris smiled. This, he thought, was possibly the one area where he had an advantage over Garrett. He silently asked the Lord to give him the right words. "I trust you have evidence to support your position?"

Garrett set his notebook aside. "I need no evidence. You can't prove an existential negative."

Brian winked at Chris, instinctively siding with the person he perceived to be the underdog. "I hope you've studied logic."

Chris acknowledged Brian's support but addressed his next question to Garrett. "Why don't you believe in God?"

"There is no proof."

"What about creation . . . the orderliness of the universe . . . the complexity of the human body?"

"Sheer chance."

Chris sorted his cards. "That's like believing that blowing up a scrap heap could produce a computer."

Garrett pushed his glasses up on the bridge of his nose. "Perhaps. But there is still no proof that God exists."

"There is no proof that anything exists. You perceive it exists. Every person lives by faith."

"Faith is intellectual suicide."

"No. When you sat down on that bed, did you check all the supports to make sure they would hold? Of course not. You sat down trusting, believing that it would function a certain way. You had faith that the bed would not collapse under you. You practice faith a hundred times a day."

Garrett was genuinely trying to give Chris's argument a fair hearing. "Using that definition, I suppose I do. Your point, then, is that since there is no proof per se, that all we have is our own perceptions?"

"Exactly. Or the testimony of reliable witnesses. The test then is whether the witness—or my perception—is reliable or not."

"If you believe in God, you must believe the authors of the Bible were reliable witnesses."

"I do."

"How can you when there is so much scholarly evidence against it?"

"The evidence against it isn't that scholarly. Scientists and so-called intellectuals keep trying, but everyone who ever attempted to disprove the Bible has either failed or converted to Christianity. The Scriptures are compelling, and if you read the whole book from front to back, you begin to understand the mind of the author."

Garrett was unwilling to concede the point. "Understanding the mind of God aside, there is a large body of evidence against the Bible. Yuring's dissertation on the myth of Jesus, the paradox of Oclasius, Hyram Noch's *The Elusive Truth Of Christianity.* How do you respond to intellectual assaults like these?"

"For thousands of years people have been trying to assault the historicity of Jesus Christ. The Jewish leaders tried to do it shortly after He rose from the dead by paying the Roman guards to lie. In the early to mid-1900s, many people thought large portions of the Old Testament were grossly inaccurate or merely a fabrication. Then the Dead Sea Scrolls were discovered and the intellectuals grew strangely silent. As the scrolls were deciphered, large portions of the book of the prophet Isaiah were shown to be letter perfect. The Bible has stood the test of time, and I'm not going to abandon my confidence in it just because some scientist says it is flawed. I don't care what he thinks his proof is."

"But what about the scientific method?"

"It has its place, but you can't treat it as if it were the pinnacle of human achievement. The scientific method is a useful tool for applications in science, but when you try to use it to verify philosophical or historical data, you get into trouble. If someone applies the method and the result contradicts the Bible, I will doubt the method long before I would doubt the Bible."

"But the method works. You still have to approach an argument logically, or it's intellectual suicide."

Chris put his cards down, the game forgotten. "Agreed. Let's put it this way. You believe in statistical probability, right?"

"Of course."

"What is the alternative to a complex universe coming together by sheer chance?"

"Creation."

"Which alternative is more probable, given the facts as we know them?"

"Creation. But it could be creation by some incredibly powerful alien being."

"God is an incredibly powerful being. I don't think 'alien' applies in this context."

"So what is your point?"

Chris stood up. "If God exists, Jesus Christ becomes possible."

"Jesus Christ is highly improbable."

"Only in a universe without God."

"But there are as many intellectual arguments against Jesus as there are against the Bible. I should know. I wrote some of them."

"Arguments are written by imperfect human beings."

Garrett looked smug. "So were the books of the Bible."

"The Bible was written by men inspired by God. I know it must seem very convenient for the purpose of argument, but everything your intellect is fighting against—the Bible, Jesus, angels, demons, all of it—becomes possible if there is a God."

Cory slammed her cards down angrily. "Will you guys knock it off? I mean it!" She looked away, embarrassed by her outburst. Chris and Brian looked shocked and quietly resumed the game, while Garrett went back to his notebook. They played on for several hours, each one afraid to say anything remotely personal, and finally broke for bed late in the evening.

Hours later—"morning" in their human life cycle—Chris

awoke with a bad taste in his mouth and knew he had been sleeping with his mouth open. He looked around the room and noticed Brian standing by the porthole looking out the window. He rose and tiptoed across the room.

"What are you doing?" he whispered.

Brian never took his eyes off the view. "Watching the sunrise."

Chris assumed he was joking until he looked out the window. The sun was rising all right, but it came up small and sudden over the dark horizon of Jupiter, illuminating the surface of Europa and taking off at a skewed angle as the moon continued in its orbit. If you weren't prepared, the effect was not unlike a roller coaster ride. He looked away from the window and sat down abruptly.

Brian smiled. "Sorry. I should have warned you."

Chris sighed, walked over to the food containers, and pulled out a self-warming tube of oatmeal. Each person was responsible for his or her own meals, which meant they more or less ate when they were hungry. As the human body burned less energy in the lower gravity of this moon, they could get by longer with less food.

The foursome passed the day as best they could—talking, reading, writing, playing games, sleeping, checking the drill's progress—but by late afternoon everyone was experiencing cabin fever. It was evening when the hose suddenly shook in its mountings.

"We're through!" Brian said, excitedly.

They turned on the pump and began running water through the distillation unit. It would take nine hours to fill the holding tank with sludge, and Brian had set the mechanism to sound a warning tone when the tank was nearly full. Once everything had been checked and doublechecked, it was agreed they would leave in the morning, and they turned out the lights and went to bed. It wasn't long before Chris could hear Brian snoring softly. The breathing from Garrett's direction was heavy and even.

Chris whispered into the darkness. "Cory?"

"Mmm. . . ."

"Why does it make you angry to talk about God?"

There was a long pause, and Chris decided he wasn't going to get an answer. But at last Cory spoke. "I had a bad experience with a youth group in high school."

"What happened?"

"I found out the youth pastor was dating my best friend. A wife and two kids and he's dating a sixteen-year-old!" she hissed. "I quit going after that."

"Did you ever give your life to Jesus?"

"If you want to call it that. I said a prayer and felt really great for about two weeks. I haven't thought about it much since then."

In the darkness, Chris could almost feel the heart of God reaching out to Cory, wanting to care for the wounded girl who had been away so long. He waited, listening for some time before he spoke again. "You know, He's never given up on you."

Cory didn't reply, so Chris assumed the conversation was over and turned on his side to go to sleep. He couldn't see the single tear roll down her cheek onto her pillow.

Chris was awakened abruptly. The pump had stopped. He opened his eyes and listened. Nothing. *Must have imagined it,* he thought, rolling over and pulling his blanket up around his neck. But then he heard it again, a faint noise, like the sound of pipes rattling. He sat up on his elbows and looked hard into the darkness. Silence.

He turned on his light, which woke Brian. "Chris, what are you doing?"

"I thought I heard something."

The hose hanging from the frame was undulating slowly back and forth over the hole. "The hose is moving."

Now Brian sat up on his elbows. "It's probably just water currents down below."

Cory murmured from her pillow. "Would you guys keep it down? Some of us are trying to sleep."

Chris left his bed and walked over to the hole. The hose moved again, brushing against the frame with a rattle. He grabbed the hose and pulled, but it didn't give. He crossed over to the retaining spool and set the winch to pull the hose up twelve inches.

"That's going to make a lot of noise," Brian warned.

"No noise!" Cory pleaded sleepily from her bed.

Chris considered the situation and decided to test his theory. He engaged the winch, the spool rotated loudly, and a foot of hose came out of the hole in the ice. No one was ready for what happened next.

The hose was suddenly, violently jerked downward tight against the frame, which shrieked and then buckled under the pressure. The safety latch on the spool tripped, freeing it to spin in the opposite direction as the hose whistled down the abyss of the hole. Chris jumped backward instinctively, tumbling over the monitoring equipment. Brian scrambled out of bed, tangled in his blanket, while Cory lay on the floor in a heap, jolted out of bed. Garrett sat up, blinking his eyes in astonishment.

"There's something down there!" Cory screamed.

Brian ran over to Chris and helped him up. He was dazed and bruised, but otherwise okay.

Cory was terrified. "Let's get out of here!"

"We can't blast off with the door open!" Brian was trying not to panic.

Chris pointed to the spool. "We're gonna run out of hose."

"Detach! Detach!"

Chris came to life, sealed the distillation unit, and fumbled with the connection at the end of the hose that was still attached. Brian punched the emergency recall switch on the spool, but the hose continued disappearing down the hole. In desperation, he grabbed a piece of pipe from the wreckage of the frame and stood before the spool, arms raised.

Chris realized too late what he had in mind. "No! Don't!"

Brian jammed the pipe into the gears for the spool. The gears wrenched and spit the pipe in the other direction, catapulting Brian over the top into the surrounding machinery.

Chris started over to Brian, but the hose ran out. There was a loud snap and the whistling stopped. He was amazed to find

71

the hose still attached. The metal in the hull began to creak under the downward pressure on the spool.

Garrett was on his feet. "Cory! Get us out of here!"

Cory ran for the cockpit, with Garrett close behind.

Chris looked at Brian, unconscious and bleeding on the floor. "Garrett! Help me with Brian!"

Garrett ignored him and threw himself into the cockpit. Chris darted across the floor and scrambled up the ladder. "Are you crazy? We've got to help Brian!"

Garrett was frantically helping Cory with the prelaunch sequence. "If the hull buckles we won't be able to take off, and we'll have four dead instead of one!" The ship shook as the engines flamed on.

Chris clenched his teeth. "I'm not leaving him." He said a quick prayer and jumped back down into the aft compartment, twisting his ankle as he landed.

"No, Chris!" Cory yelled. "I may have broken the seal already!"

As if to confirm her warning, air started hissing out the hole in the floor. Chris limped over to Brian and threw his unconscious friend over his shoulder. The pain in his ankle was excruciating, but he focused on the door to the cockpit with every fiber of his being. A burst of adrenaline coursed through his veins and suddenly he was running. The air was already getting thin as he jumped up to the second rung and climbed with one hand to the cockpit door. Garrett grabbed Brian and pulled him through, and Chris collapsed on the floor inside the cockpit.

"Close the door!" Chris gritted, holding his ankle.

While Garrett punched the controls for the door, Cory reached over her head with both hands, grabbed two silver handles recessed in the ceiling, gave each a quarter turn, and pulled down hard. "This is it!"

The emergency boosters flamed on and the shuttle lurched upward, gaining several thousand feet in a matter of seconds. Chris was thrown hard against the floor, and the others in the cockpit nearly passed out from the acceleration. The boosters shut off automatically, and the ship hurtled up and away from

Europa. Cory shook her head to clear her mind and fired the main thrusters briefly, bringing them into a high orbit. She checked her instruments, plotted a course for Io, and engaged the autopilot. All was quiet for a moment.

Cory looked toward the door. "How are we doing back there?"

Garrett stood in the doorway to survey the compartment. "Lots of debris. Looks like we lost some of the equipment. We got the hose back."

"How'd we get the hose back?"

"I think Brian hit the emergency recall."

"Is the hole sealed?"

"We're holding pressure."

She manipulated the emergency controls that closed the bottom hatch by remote, just to make sure, and continued repressurizing the aft compartment. Chris looked over at Brian. Blood was oozing from a gash in his forehead.

"Brian doesn't look too good," Chris said thickly. He still felt woozy.

"We need to get him another blanket. He may go into shock," Garrett said.

"There are some extra blankets back there." Chris jerked his thumb toward the aft compartment.

Cory checked her gauges. "Everything looks pretty good up here. We can go back anytime."

"Stay put, Chris," said Garrett preemptively. "Cory, come with me."

The twosome climbed down and began putting the aft compartment back in order. The wreckage from the collapsed frame and two of the monitors apparently had been blown out through the hatch during blastoff, but everything else was accounted for.

Garrett examined the rod at the end of the hose. The drill bit at the end of the rod was gone. And there was something else. "Look at this."

Cory maneuvered over to the spool, her eyes widening. "Are those *teethmarks?*"

"I think so." They stared at each other for a moment, imaginations running wild.

Garrett shuddered and let go of the rod, and the two of them quickly finished securing the last of the equipment and floating debris. They returned to the cockpit and Garrett took a look at Brian. Chris was nursing his now-swollen ankle, rocking slightly with pain, and watching Brian, who still hadn't moved. Garrett met his gaze.

"You really believe that stuff, don't you?"

Chris was nonplussed. "What stuff?"

"You know. God. Loving your neighbor as yourself. All of that." Chris raised his eyebrows in surprise and Garrett continued. "I minored in religion as an undergraduate."

Chris closed his eyes with fatigue and nodded. "There's another good one: 'Greater love has no one than this, than to lay down one's life for his friends.'"

Garrett looked at Brian. "I'm glad it wasn't me."

"I'd have done it for you, too."

CHAPTER 6

Chris woke up in his own bed at noon the next day, feeling greatly refreshed but still stiff and sore. No sign of Manny. He showered and dressed, had a quick lunch, and went to his afternoon classes. He checked his messages before dinner and was pleasantly surprised to discover that his father and brother would be arriving in just over a week.

After dinner, he limped straight over to the lab. He was surprised to find the distiller already taken apart. Then he noticed an even bigger surprise.

"Brian!"

"Hi, Chris." Brian sported a thick bandage on his forehead.

"What are you doing here?"

"They said if I took it easy, I was free to leave."

Cory and Garrett sat at the worktable, looking decidedly dejected. "What's wrong?"

Garrett's voice was flat. "Cory dug up some additional research on superheavy elements and conductivity."

"Let me guess. We got the wrong source material?" Garrett shook his head so Chris went on. "Not enough source material?"

Garrett interrupted. "The post production process requires a forty-five-pound slab of pure selenium."

"Forty-five pounds? Every time I don't read the instructions something like this happens. I don't suppose they stock it on campus."

"We checked."

"Could we manufacture it here?"

"It would be faster to order it from Earth."

Without warning, the door flung open and Dr. Whitlock stormed in. "I heard you were back. I want to know what the . . . Garrett, who are these people?"

"This is my team, Lloyd. Team, this is Doctor Lloyd Whitlock, Director of Doctoral Studies."

"We never discussed this," Dr. Whitlock said dangerously.

"Surely you didn't expect me to do it alone?"

"Outside, Mr. Alger."

"Lloyd . . ."

"Now!"

Garrett followed Dr. Whitlock out into the hall. The door closed behind them, but they stepped into full view of the monitor.

"Are you crazy?" Dr. Whitlock yelled.

Garrett backed away. "Relax. They don't know anything about the deal with Henderson."

"I don't care! They shouldn't be here at all."

"I was just trying to meet his schedule."

"I told you we were no longer building a sentient machine!"

"How do you know about that?" Garrett asked incredulously.

"I am not grotesquely stupid, Garrett. The converter station is short a few neural circuits."

Garrett looked at the floor. "I can't believe they found it."

"You fool! Why didn't you order them from Earth?"

Garrett was finally angry. "Because of Henderson's ridiculous deadline!"

"The contract states explicitly that he needs a heuristic battle machine for a major procurement, not some sideshow freak machine for your personal amusement. If he doesn't have it, he's out several million dollars."

"If word of our arrangement gets out, he'll be out a lot more than that."

Dr. Whitlock's expression hardened. "That's why he's on his way here right now."

76

The blood drained from Garrett's face. "Henderson? Here?"

Inside the lab, his three teammates were wishing they could read lips. Gathered around the monitor like children, they were trying hard to follow the conversation.

"What do you suppose he did?" Cory wanted to know.

"Well," Chris replied, "we were a big surprise, that's for sure."

Brian was puzzled. "I know Lloyd. I've never seen him carry on so."

After several minutes, Dr. Whitlock left as abruptly as he had arrived. Garrett entered the lab, looking like a whipped dog. "Sorry about that."

Brian put a hand on his shoulder and helped him sit down. "What was that all about?"

Garrett hesitated, uncomfortable with an outright lie. "He's just mad because I didn't tell him about the team."

Chris was hoping they wouldn't have to quit. "Did he stop the project?"

"On the contrary, we have even less time to finish than before."

"What does Lloyd have to do with it?" Brian asked.

Garrett was quiet for a moment. "There's a department fundraiser next month. He was hoping we could impress some people into making heavy donations. But I don't suppose there's much chance of that now."

Cory didn't want to quit, either. "There's got to be a faster way to get the selenium."

Brian moved to the computer screen. "Aren't there bacteria that excrete useful products?"

Garrett nodded. "Yes. But it takes billions of them. I'm sure they have some in the biology department, but I still think it would take too long. Cory, you have friends over there. They must have some way of doing it."

Cory was not optimistic. "I've tried bargaining with these guys before. Even if they do have what we need, there's no way they're going to give us anything."

Brian looked sourly at Garrett. "It would have to be the one place you don't have any connections."

Inspiration lit up Chris's face. "I do!"

* * *

Chris limped all the way across campus and up three flights of stairs to his room. Manny wasn't there. Out of breath, he took off for the Biological Sciences building. The guard at the front desk hadn't seen Manny, so Chris decided to try the recreational center.

After a hasty search of the ground floor, Chris found Manny in the basement in one of the workout rooms. Chris grabbed him by the arm and dragged him into the hallway. "We have to talk."

Manny followed him down the hall to a deserted portion of the lower level, complaining all the way. "At least let me change my clothes!"

Once Chris was sure there was no one around, he politely told his friend to shut up. "I needed to talk to you in private. I have a proposition for you."

"I'm listening."

"I need a forty-five-pound slab of pure selenium, and I'm willing to bet the biology department has . . ."

"Forget it."

". . . bacteria, or some other oddball method for manufacturing it."

"I said forget it."

"But you haven't heard my offer."

"There's nothing you could offer that would make me break the rules like that."

"Who said anything about breaking the rules? I don't want to break your stupid rules. I want a slab of selenium!"

"We can't use the things in the lab for personal benefit."

"Did I mention I need forty-five pounds of it?"

"I'm going to the locker room."

Manny turned to leave. Chris grabbed his shoulder and spun him around.

"Look at you," Manny said disgustedly. "This is getting to be an obsession."

"Will you shut up and listen to me? While we were on Europa, we drilled through the ice to the liquid sea."

"You're kidding."

"No. Something under the ice grabbed the hose and nearly tore the ship apart."

Manny's jaw dropped. Clearly, Chris had his full attention now. "I have a metal rod with teethmarks, and maybe even a few tissue samples."

Manny closed his mouth. "I'll talk to the head of the department tomorrow."

Two days later, a forty-five-pound slab of pure selenium was delivered to Garrett's lab.

Chris awoke from a troubled sleep. Manny was snoring in the opposite bed and a quick look at his chronometer told him dawn was still an hour away. He knew he wouldn't be able to get back to sleep, and his first class wasn't until ten, so he threw on a pair of sweats and tennis shoes and hobbled over to Folsom Hall. His ankle was mending quickly.

The halls were deserted, as they should be at such an hour, and when he entered Garrett's lab, he found it unoccupied as well. He half-expected to find Garrett slumped over one of the computer terminals. Strewn across the large conference table were the main pieces of the skeleton. The pieces for the hands and fingers lay on one workbench, and the parts for the feet were on another. The rib cage had been molded in a single piece, and because of its size, lay on a towel on the floor.

Chris sat down at a workbench and began working on the hands. Each of the joints was fashioned in such a way that they would mimic the normal range of motion for the corresponding human joint. Chris had spent the last day and a half organizing all the bones and preparing them to receive Cory's bioelectric constructions. She had been working long hours, building hundreds of tiny motors and all the necessary connections which would allow the brain to direct the movements of the body.

Piece by piece, joining and locking each joint with care, Chris slowly assembled the right hand, then the left, and carried them over to the table, aligning them with the ulna and radius of the lower arms. He checked his chronometer, thinking only twenty minutes had passed, and was shocked to find that he was about to be late for his ten o'clock class.

He hurried out of the lab and down the stairs, nearly running into one of the doctoral students, and dashed out the front door as best he could to the second building on the right. Reaching the classroom with a minute to spare, he was able to borrow a piece of paper and pen from one of his classmates before the professor stood up and addressed the class.

"Good morning. I want to give you as much time to complete the examination as possible, so we will begin immediately."

Chris had missed class twice this week, hadn't read the assigned chapters, and hadn't taken the time to borrow anyone's notes. The professor began passing out test booklets and Chris realized, with a sinking feeling in the pit of his stomach, that for the first time in six years, he was about to fail a test.

Cory arrived at the lab early in the afternoon, and the first thing she noticed was the newly assembled hands lying on the table. Had she been the type, she would have squealed with delight, but instead she calmly admired the workmanship, then gathered her equipment, sat down, and immediately began attaching tiny motors, gears, and cables to the shiny, blue extremities.

Garrett came in some time later, carrying a stack of reports and a couple of books. He set the reading material on one of the least cluttered workbenches, and peered over Cory's right shoulder

Cory stopped working. "I don't mean to be difficult, but I wish you'd stop doing that."

"You mean looking over your shoulder? Sorry. It's a bad habit I picked up student teaching."

"No problem. I don't mind you watching, but it's hard to concentrate with you perched there like that."

Garrett moved to one side and sat down beside her. "Better?"

"Much. Chris must have been in here this morning. I found both hands assembled."

"I know. I came in here before meeting Brian at the library. Chris does nice work."

Cory switched tools like a surgeon and kept working. "What were you doing at the library?"

"Research. I wanted to find out what the latest artificial intelligence studies had to offer. This is going to be an incredibly complex mechanism, and I'm not too proud to listen to someone else's conclusions."

Brian came in just then, carrying his own stack of papers. "I promised Teresa we would have these papers back in two days. We're not really supposed to take them out of the library. Hi, Cory."

"H'lo, Brian. What do you think of the hands?"

"Shaping up nicely. Those motors are Mechler-graduated, aren't they?"

Cory was surprised. "Yes. How did you know that?"

"My doctoral thesis had a chapter on robotics. Mechler had recently published his findings, so I incorporated it into my work. This poor, illegitimate beast is going to be strong, isn't he?"

Garrett stood up. "We don't want him in the shop for repairs every other day, but that's why we're taking such extraordinary safety precautions. The lesson of Victor Frankenstein was not lost on me."

Brian smiled. "Afraid the faculty will burn you to death in a windmill?"

"Actually, the scenario I am trying to avoid is the one in which the creature destroys the creator. We will adhere to very stringent procedures when we enter the testing phase."

"I should hope so. Does anyone know where Chris is?"

Garrett checked a schedule tacked to a bulletin board. "He has an afternoon class which will be over in about fifteen minutes. Apparently he actually attended class today. How is the program coming?"

Brian sat down at the computer terminal and keyed in a series

81

of commands. "I was going to do a first run tonight, during off-peak hours. The program should take about four and a half hours to run. I should be able to begin testing the mind in the morning."

Garrett looked concerned. "You are using a secure area, I assume?"

"I'm having the information for the mind downloaded into my desktop system, which is locked in my office. I have the only key, and I removed all the communications connections from the system. It's about as secure as you can get."

Cory interrupted. "Excuse me? Could one of you give me a hand?"

Brian picked up the other mechanical hand off the table and handed it to her. Cory was not impressed. "Funny. Garrett, would you mind holding this connection in place while I lock it down? Brian is malfunctioning again."

Garrett picked up a tool and held the connection in place. "I should take him into the shop. He's due for a tune-up."

Brian chuckled. "You two are always so serious, I feel obligated to lighten things up now and then."

Neither responded, as they were concentrating on coordinating their movements so the connection would be mounted in the right place. After a half minute of holding their breath, the connection was complete, but the next series required the same kind of gyrations.

Chris came in part way through their work but received acknowledgment only from Brian. "Hi. Don't bother. They're working on some dicey connections."

Chris was amused. *"Dicey?"*

"You know—difficult, hazardous. Popular in late twentieth century detective novels."

"You read detective novels?"

Brian shrugged. "A professor's got to have a hobby."

Garrett and Cory worked for another twenty minutes, and by the time they were finished their hands were cramping. Garrett sat back and took a deep breath, and Cory stood up and stretched her legs and her fingers. Chris walked over for a good look at their handiwork. If he squinted his eyes, Cory's connections looked a little like tendons.

Brian followed his gaze. "We're going to have a heck of a time making the exterior look like smooth skin."

"Don't worry. I got it 'covered,'" joked Chris. He produced another carrying case from a corner of the lab and hoisted it onto the table. "Have a look."

Brian walked over. Inside was a sizable collection of foam constructions in varying shapes and sizes. "What is this stuff?"

"These are the pieces which will go over the skeleton, once Cory's work is done."

"You mean, this stuff is intended to simulate muscle and subcutaneous flesh? How did you do it?"

"The metallurgy shop has an injection molding machine. The machine is interfaced to the mainframe. This was actually easier than the skeleton."

Garrett peered over Brian's shoulder. "Remind me to send the metallurgy department a dozen roses."

With the help of Brian and Garrett, Chris was able to finish the skeleton by late evening. Cory never stopped working on her connections, and by the time they quit for the night, everyone was ravenous. They agreed to have dinner together at *The All-Nighter*.

As they waited for their robot waiter to bring the food, Chris noticed how tired everyone looked.

"You guys look awful."

"Have you looked in a mirror recently?" Cory asked.

Chris smiled weakly. "I deserved that. I don't know how long I can keep this up."

Garrett rubbed his eyes. "Just another week or two, I hope. Then you can get on with your lives."

Brian took a drink from his glass of water. "Garrett, why are we doing this? Really."

Garrett knew from the look on Brian's face that he had guessed there was more to the story than what the group had been told at the beginning. "I can't tell you, but it's a special project for Whitlock."

"Why can't you tell us?"

"He's got a contract with an outside party."

"But if we already know the parameters . . ."

"You don't. There is more to the project than what I've told you. It's much more complicated than I can get into right now. I was afraid if I told you the whole story you wouldn't want to be involved. And I very much needed you to be involved."

"You should have let us make that determination," Brian chided softly.

Cory was hurt. "You lied to us."

Brian held up a hand and continued. "Nothing is going to be accomplished by making accusations. What was the original project supposed to be?"

"That's the part I can't discuss. Look, I should have told you about this up front. I was wrong, and I'm sorry I didn't. But we are so close. I wouldn't blame you if you quit right now, but I hope you won't. If for no other reason than you want to see if we can do it."

Brian looked down at his hands. Cory and Chris looked away, not sure how to react. Garrett leaned forward in his chair, a beseeching look on his face. "Please."

The plea caught everyone off guard. For Garrett to beg, this had to be something he wanted desperately. Brian scrutinized Garrett solemnly.

"If I didn't know Lloyd Whitlock, I'd probably get out right now. But I'd be lying if I said I didn't want to see this thing through."

Chris still wasn't sure what to think. "It kind of hurts, Garrett. Of all people, I figured you would be straight with us."

"For that, I am very sorry. I got into this without thinking it through very well, I'm afraid. I promise you, when it's all over I'll fill you in on all the details—or most of them, anyway."

Chris nodded slowly, and Garrett looked at Cory, who shrugged. "It's no skin off my nose. I'm in this for the extra credit."

Garrett looked pained, but the expression passed as quickly as it had come. Chris wondered briefly if Garrett had feelings

84

for Cory but dismissed the thought as preposterous. Their food arrived a short time later, and they were saved the agony of trying to make conversation.

At the end of the meal, they went their separate way, each one wondering if he had made the right decision.

Chris got up early on Saturday, planning to go straight to the lab. He had finished assembling the metal skeleton the night before and wanted to do some final testing on the electrical relays Cory had installed. He showered quickly, dressed, and was just about to take off, when he realized Manny was watching him from his bed. With a pang of guilt, he spoke lightly from the doorway.

"Felicitations, squalid Mandrake. Didst thou enjoy protracted unconsciousness?"

"We have a game this morning. Not that you care, of course." There was resignation in Manny's voice.

"I'm really sorry. It should only be a few more days." Chris felt terrible.

Manny sat up, genuine concern on his face. "Did you ever ask God if He wanted you to do this?"

"I think so."

"Did you ask Him if you were supposed to keep doing it?" Chris was quiet. "You got what you thought was direction from Him, and then ran off without once looking back, didn't you?"

"I guess maybe I did. Look, I can't deal with this right now. Can we talk about this later?"

Manny looked away. "Sure."

Chris walked out the door and downstairs to breakfast, feeling lousy. Everything he was doing seemed to be out of character. It was as if he were acting out a role in someone else's play, and he didn't like the part.

As Chris closed the door, Manny decided he'd had enough. He called Marshall and then Leigh, asking them to meet him in the lobby right away. Manny threw on some sweats, grabbed his laundry bag, and hurried down to meet his friends. Marshall showed up first, looking annoyed, and Leigh was not far behind.

Manny explained that they were going to help someone who was in trouble.

Chris sat by himself in the cafeteria, partly because there wasn't anyone he knew very well, partly because he felt like being alone. Unfortunately, he wasn't very good company at the moment, and the only person he had to talk to was himself. *Life was much less complicated before I met Garrett,* he thought. *If I had it to do over, would I accept Garrett's offer? Probably, but I definitely would have done some things differently. Like, spend more time with Manny, and not so much in the lab. And study more.*

But he hadn't done things differently, and now his friends had hurt feelings and his grades were well on their way to becoming a disaster. It seemed he had two choices, neither of which was particularly appealing. He could quit the project and leave Garrett high and dry. That would mean letting down some people he cared about very much. Or he could stick it out, finish the project, quit the football team, and fail his courses. That would also mean letting down some people he cared about very much. No matter how he looked at it, someone wasn't going to like him very much when this was all over.

Chris left half his breakfast uneaten and walked out of the cafeteria. As he stepped from the lobby onto the sidewalk, a pair of strong arms grabbed him from behind and a cloth bag was thrown over his head. He had heard horror stories of students being stripped to their underwear, covered with shaving cream, and stuffed in a sleeping bag to be left on the doorstep of a sorority. At times like these, he was not too proud to beg.

"Guys, whatever you're planning, don't do it! I have money. . . ."

His assailants weren't talking, so he tried to figure out which direction they were headed. Across campus . . . they were already past the sorority houses . . . the fountain. They were headed toward the fountain. Chris had never tried swimming inside a cloth bag and didn't intend to start now. He put everything he had into a squirming break for freedom. The arms holding him might as well have been made of steel.

86

"Marshall? Is that you?"

Nothing. They walked on past the fountain, and Chris breathed yet another sigh of relief. He was feeling bruised from the strong grip on his arms, and he hoped they would reach their destination soon, even if he wound up face to face with a can of shaving cream. Voices. He heard voices. Lots of them. The Student Union Building? Why . . ."

He was deposited unceremoniously on a hard bench and the cloth sack removed.

"Manfred! What are you doing?"

Manny smiled. "Saving you from yourself."

"By sticking my head in your stinky laundry bag?"

"Desperate times require desperate measures."

They were in a booth in the lounge of the Student Union Building, and Leigh and Marshall were seated across from him.

"We're here to make sure you eat a decent breakfast before knocking yourself out in the lab," Leigh said, picking up a menu.

All of a sudden, Chris realized what a rotten friend he had been lately. Here he had been ignoring his friends for the past few weeks, and they had thrown a party for him. He picked up a menu self-consciously, unable to meet their eyes. He folded and unfolded the card awkwardly and stared at the table. "Listen, I've been kind of a jerk lately, and I'm sorry."

"Kind of?" Manny asked, arching his eyebrows.

"Okay, a humongous jerk. I think my priorities got kind of bent out of shape."

"I'll say!" Leigh peeked over her menu.

"Look. I won't even go to the lab today. My dad's ship is due in sometime late this afternoon. We'll play our game and then we can all go and storm the rec center after lunch."

Manny thumped his hand on the table. "Now you're talking!"

They ordered a continental breakfast and ate quickly, Marshall devouring almost an entire basket of rolls. When they were finished, Chris left the lounge under his own power, and the group walked back toward the dorm. When they started across the field, Marshall put his arm around Chris's shoulders.

"So tell me, little fellah. Was it worth it?"

"Was what worth it?"

"This whole gig with Garrett Alger."

"I'll let you know in a few days."

When they reached the dorm, they returned to their rooms to get ready for their game. With the protection of his athletic shoes, Chris was willing to risk his ankle. As they headed for the football field, Manny drew close to Chris and spoke conspiratorially.

"Incidentally, we made some preliminary findings on those teethmarks from Europa."

Chris was all ears. "Yes?"

"Evidence suggests, however implausible, that the creature is of Earth origin."

"How can that be?"

"Our best guess is that it is descended from microbes or something bigger left behind by some of the earliest explorers. They probably drilled indiscriminately, without much care for what they were leaving behind. Whatever they deposited must have liked the warm, mineral-rich water. It was fruitful and multiplied."

Somehow the idea that the shuttle had nearly been destroyed by a giant amoeba struck Chris as funny and he laughed. "Next time I go fishing, remind me to take a bigger boat."

The passenger ship was in an elliptical orbit around Io, due to the strong pull from Jupiter. Ryan had his face pressed against the viewport in their cabin, but because of the odd orbit, Jupiter was only visible for a few seconds every twenty minutes.

The Grahams's cabin was all buttoned up and their bags by the door, waiting for word on the debarkation shuttle from the spaceport. Nathan was looking forward to being on solid ground again. Ryan, who had finished most of his school work, couldn't wait to run wild.

The captain announced the arrival of the shuttle, and the Grahams moved out into the hallway toward the main hatch, almost colliding with a tall man with a square jaw and expensive leather shoes. They apologized and moved on, not noticing the look of shock on the man's face. He ducked down the hallway into one of the cabins.

Lash Wagner was never without a pair of genuine leather shoes. Clothing made of animal skin was no longer used by most civilized people, but he liked the idea of "wearing death on my feet," as he called it. His face had a menacing cast with broad high cheekbones, his mouth a cruel slash. He had neither been beaten as a child nor deprived of an education; there had been no trauma, no hardship, no illness to account for his sociopathic behavior. He simply took no thought for the welfare of others. Somewhere along the way, he had found there was good money in killing if one could get past the guilt. Wagner's guilt was long dead—murdered with his first victim—along with any shred of human warmth or compassion.

Morgan Henderson had discovered him on a business trip several years back and hired him to do away with his partner. The job was done so well, Lash had been hired permanently. They hated each other as they hated everyone, but Morgan had much dirty work to be done, and Lash welcomed the money.

Lash leaned up against the wall of the cabin, waiting for Morgan to notice him. Morgan Henderson sat at the table trying to keep current with his business affairs. Shrewd and ruthless, he was known for his insatiable will to win.

Lash took out a switchblade with exaggerated slowness and started cleaning his fingernails. "Nathan Graham is on board."

Morgan Henderson looked up with contempt from the stack of papers in front of him. "You only just noticed? I've known for a week. Where is he?"

"I ran into him and his son—I think—in the hallway."

"Did he recognize you?"

"I don't think so."

"You were lucky. He may have a file on you. He's good. He's very good."

"Do you think he knows about us?" Lash ran his finger along the blade, as if checking the smooth edge.

Morgan replied, "If he did, he would have had us arrested by now. No. I think he's probably investigating the theft and brought his boy along to check out the academy."

"Then there's nothing to worry about." Lash closed his knife and put it back inside his jacket.

"Of course there is, you idiot! The trail from those circuits to me isn't very long, and I assure you he will find it. There is much at stake here, Mr. Wagner. I can't afford loose ends."

"There are many ways to die in space, Mr. Henderson."

Chris met Nathan and Ryan as they walked off the ramp from the shuttle. Smiling, he gave his dad a big hug. But when he turned to Ryan, his smile faded.

"Mom told me you grew," Chris said, somewhat taken aback.

Ryan was uncomfortable under his brother's scrutiny. "I did."

Chris was no longer sure he could best his not-so-little brother in a fair fight. "Just remember, youth and skill will always lose out to old age and treachery."

Ryan laughed, and the two embraced as if they'd never been apart. The three of them walked out of the spaceport and into the late afternoon sun. The effect of the fresh air and lush scenery was almost magical. Tension lines in their faces eased, their pace slowed slightly, breathing came easier and deeper.

Chris put his arm around his brother's shoulder. "Good job on the tournament."

Ryan smiled at the unexpected praise. "I would have taken first, but the guy switched gambits on me."

"Switched gambits?"

"He used a classic Karnikov Ruse—a nasty, and very deceptive, three-layer offense—but he changed the last move. I should have seen it coming."

"You just can't trust some people."

"How are your studies?" Nathan asked.

Chris hesitated. "Pretty good. I'm having a little trouble keeping up 'cause I've been working on a special project with one of the doctoral students."

"What kind of project?"

"Can't say. We're all under nondisclosure."

Dr. Graham hated to give the speech but did so anyway. "You realize, of course, that if it comes down to a choice between the project and your studies. . . ."

"Don't worry. I haven't lost *all* perspective."

On their way to the guest accommodations in Chris's dorm, they bumped into Leigh coming back from a workout. She aimed a wet towel at Chris before she realized he had company.

"Whoops! Sorry about that."

His shirt was soaked. "Think nothing of it."

"Aren't you going to introduce me?"

"Leigh Quintana, this is my father, Nathan Graham."

She shook Nathan's hand, smiling. "Glad to finally meet you."

"Likewise," Nathan replied, returning the smile.

"And my brother Ryan."

Leigh's eyes twinkled. "Very cute. Looks like he got all the looks. Well, gotta run. Nice to meet you both!"

Chris threw back the towel as she turned to go. Ryan watched dreamily.

"All right, Romeo." Chris gave his brother a playful shove. "Keep moving. And try not to step on your tongue."

"Are all the girls like that here?"

"Dream on, lover boy."

Nathan sounded thoughtful. "She seems to be a nice girl. You two ever gone out?"

"You mean on a date? No way."

"Why not?"

"We're too good friends. I don't want to ruin it."

"Your mother and I were good friends before we went out."

"Yeah, yeah. You were twenty-four years old, too. I can wait." They were at the door. Chris produced a key. "This is your room. I'm in three-fifteen. Dinner's at six downstairs. I'll meet you there."

With that, Chris headed out of the dorm and jogged slowly across the field to Folsom Hall. Outside the door to Garrett's lab was a large package. Scrawled on the front in black marker was his name, and nothing else. He dragged the package into the lab and opened it with a pocket knife. Inside was a stack of sheets two feet square, made of flesh-colored material so much like human skin it was hard to tell the difference.

"It better be hard to tell the difference," Chris said to himself. "It's going to cost me three months of volunteer work at the medical center."

The sheets of synthetic skin were made of a cellulose derivative and used by the medical center for skin replacement on patients who had been burned or scarred in an accident. Because of the number of laboratory experiments conducted on campus each year, burns from chemical spills were the most common. The synthetic skin functioned like a patch, and though it wouldn't regenerate if torn, it was much tougher than real skin.

Cory had finished her connections the previous afternoon and spent the rest of the day testing and cross-checking her work to make sure every subsystem was fully functional. The machine was lying on the table where she had left it, face down with one arm over the skull.

Chris moved the arm down to the side of the torso, turned the skull toward him, and pried the teeth apart with his fingers. Inside the mouth was perhaps the most impressive piece of bioelectric engineering he had ever seen. The machine's tongue was shaped like a human one but consisted of dozens of tiny motors and pulleys, each subsystem corresponding to the appropriate muscle.

The eyes stared blankly out of the blue metal of the skull. The motors controlling the eyes were not as complex, and the eyes themselves were standard optical input devices, with a prosthetic exterior. The ears were even less of a problem, since most of the computers on campus were equipped with voice input devices. It had been a simple task to install two of the devices into the sides of the skull.

Chris grabbed the machine by the shoulders and turned it over onto its back, making a considerable clattering in the process. With the carrying case on the table, he pulled out a map of the human body and began putting the injection molded muscle and flesh pieces in their assigned locations, bolting them to the skeleton. He was impressed by the realism of the striations in the muscle. The foam was so hard that the striations might even show through the synthetic skin, like a body builder.

His chronometer beeped at 5:50, to remind him to meet his dad and brother for dinner. All the muscle and flesh pieces were in place, except for the hands and the feet. The machine now gave the impression of a man who had been skinned. The sight was unsettling, and Chris was glad the foam was colored beige, not a shade of red.

Garrett wanted to begin testing tomorrow night. If Chris was going to finish bolting the pieces in place and gluing on the skin, he would have to work all night. He would probably miss morning classes and be worthless for the afternoon as well, but he didn't see any alternative. The hardest part was going to be sitting through dinner with his dad asking all kinds of difficult questions about how his studies were going.

He left the lab, already irritated with his father at the prospect of an interrogation, and walked to the cafeteria with his hands shoved into the bottom of his pockets. Wishing he were somewhere else, Chris spotted his dad and brother at the end of the food line.

They made small talk, and Chris was beginning to think he could avoid the subject of studies altogether. But it was not to be.

"You look tired. Been studying hard?" Nathan asked when they reached a table.

Chris felt the knot in his stomach tighten. "It's this special project. It seems like all I ever do anymore is work in the lab."

"Are you falling behind in your studies?"

"You could say that. But it won't be for long. We're almost through." Fatigue made his temper short, and he wished his dad would drop the subject.

"How soon?"

Chris gritted his teeth. "One or two weeks."

"You can drop a couple of grade points in one or two weeks."

Chris lost it. "Just get off my back!"

He stood up and stormed out of the cafeteria, leaving Nathan and Ryan with stunned looks on their faces. Chris knew he wouldn't be able to concentrate if he went back to the lab, so he ran up to his room and flopped on the bed.

Dad was right, he knew. But if he quit now, they would miss Garrett's deadline. The thought of letting Garrett down made him feel even worse and he got up, ready to head back to the lab. Then there was a knock at the door. He opened it to find his dad.

"May I come in?"

"Sure."

Nathan entered and closed the door behind him. Chris sat on Manny's bed and his dad sat across from him.

Chris spoke first. "Listen, I'm sorry for getting angry. I've been under a lot of pressure."

"I'm sorry, too. I should know better than to pry. You're not a kid anymore. I just forget sometimes."

"Things will work out. One way or another the project will end, and I'll work my fingers to the bone trying to get caught up. But I made a commitment, and I intend to see it through."

"And I respect you for that. I'm just worried about you, that's all. If there's any way I can help, just ask."

"Thanks, Dad. I just may take you up on that."

Nathan stood up and walked to the door. "Why don't you get some sleep?"

"You don't know how good that sounds."

"But?"

"But I have a long night ahead."

Nathan bit his lip to keep from saying the first thing that came to his head. "Then do the very best work you can. And don't kill yourself."

"Thanks."

Chris walked over for a hug, and then Nathan let himself out.

Garrett was alone in the lab. On the table in front of him, like a patient stretched out for surgery, was the machine. Its back was laid open, revealing the sublayer of foam muscle, layers of motor systems, and glimpses of shiny blue skeleton beneath it all. The team wasn't due to assemble for another hour.

Garrett had found Chris putting the finishing touches on the dermal layer, early that morning. Garrett worked alongside him until nine, preparing the brain for attachment to the brain stem. Once Chris left to get some sleep, Garrett worked feverishly without a break to complete the attachment.

Garrett had originally chosen a generically male form arbitrarily, and named him SHONN earlier in the week, for Sentient Heuristic Organic Neural Network. Chris had joked that once they tested him, they might have to rename him STUBS, for Silly Totally Useless Bucket of Scrap. Garrett had not been amused.

SHONN's voice was male, and if you looked at his face too long, you had the disquieting feeling that it was, well, too generic—more than a mannequin but somehow less than human. Cory had recalculated the cumulative energy available to SHONN's limbs and concluded he might be stronger than anticipated. With this in mind, they had built motion inhibitors into a standby enclosure, a vertical booth where he would spend his idle time.

Once Chris and Cory had completed the enclosure, Brian had programmed some additional controls on the mainframe. During the alpha and beta testing phases, SHONN would be linked to the mainframe for added security. Only when everything was operating within acceptable parameters would they disconnect him from the mainframe and try an unlinked field test.

Brian had been testing the mind on the mainframe for over a week, looking for a personality, language, memories, experiences, adding additional data where necessary and assembling all the information into a single file on the mainframe. Once SHONN was activated, they would begin loading the information into his brain. Only then could they begin trying to determine if the machine was "alive" or not.

The lab door opened without warning and in walked Dr. Whitlock, followed by Morgan Henderson and Lash Wagner.

"Good evening, Doctor Alger."

Garrett looked up, his expression of exhaustion quickly turning to one of fear. "M-M-Mr. Henderson."

Henderson walked slowly around the room. "So. This is where it all happens." He fingered the equipment as he passed by. "I'm afraid I don't know much about science. All I really know about is taking care of business." He reached the end of the worktable and stopped. "And right now, I'm worried that *this*," he slammed his fist down on SHONN's leg, "this little piece of science is going to cost me some big business."

"Please, Mr. Henderson, let me explain . . ."

"*Shut up!* I don't want to hear it. You had your chance, Doctor Alger. You could have been a rich man. I wanted the perfect killing machine, but you used my money to build this . . . this . . ." He erupted in a string of expletives and kicked several chairs across the room.

But as quickly as he had turned violent, he regained his composure. "You're fired, Doctor Alger," he said coldly, nose-to-nose with Garrett. "The next ship is in one week. You have exactly that long to get this . . . thing ready for transport. I'll finish it myself. In the meantime, this is my associate, Lash Wagner. He has proven very useful in guarding my investments."

Lash Wagner walked over to a tray of chemicals and picked up a container of acid. He opened it, pretending to lose his balance, and then he dropped it deliberately. Acid splashed onto the floor and one of the cabinets with a hiss, eating through the door of the cabinet.

"Sorry about the mess, Doctor Alger. I guess Mr. Wagner isn't very good with science either. I'd be careful who I let in here in the future. Someone could get hurt."

He walked out of the lab, followed by Wagner and Dr. Whitlock, who only shook his head. Garrett was beyond caring. He folded his arms and put his head down.

That was how Brian found him when he arrived minutes later. "I just stopped by to say I'm going to be a little late tonight."

Garrett's voice was hollow. "Fine. I expect we'll begin testing tonight."

Brian noticed the acid burns on the floor. "What happened over here?"

"I dropped one of the containers. Don't worry, I'm fine."

"You sound terrible."

"I've just been working too hard. Go on. I'll see you later."

In the lab that evening, Garrett, Cory, and Chris started up SHONN for testing. With his head open, they began with reflexes. After repatching the connections to the right leg and hip, they enabled the optical circuits, aural receptors, and speech center. Preliminary calibration complete, they established a direct link to the mainframe to begin experience engineering. The brain could not be programmed like a normal computer. Events had to be transmitted to memory in sequence or the data interrelationships would be confused. Information could be stored at a rate of one year every ten minutes.

Brian arrived at one hour, fifty minutes, when they suspended the information loading. No one was exactly sure how to proceed next.

Brian spoke hesitantly. "SHONN, can you hear me?"

The synthetic mouth opened, and that mechanical wonder of a tongue came to life, turning the droning sound emanating from the throat into speech.

"Yes."

Whoops and shouts erupted from the team. Even Garrett was grinning and slapping everyone on the back. After a few moments, Brian raised his hand for silence.

"Do you know who I am?"

"You . . . are . . . Brian . . . Mee-la-skoh." The speech was stilted but clear.

Cory was fascinated. "How does it know your name?"

"I put all of our faces into the image recognition buffer, and cross-referenced them with our names. I programmed it to respond to the name SHONN."

Chris could hardly contain his excitement. "SHONN, do you know who I am?"

The machine turned to face him. "The hair is different, but

I estimate a ninety-four percent probability that you are Chris Graham."

Chris grinned at Brian. "What was that bit about the hair?"

"I used your yearbook picture from last year."

Garrett addressed the machine. "SHONN, how do you feel?"

"I feel fine."

Garrett raised his eyebrows at Brian, but Brian shook his head. "Conventional response."

"This is going to be tougher than I thought," Garrett replied.

The team members began pumping SHONN with questions: Why is the sky blue? How many eggs in a dozen? Who was the sixteenth President of the United States? until they couldn't think of any more to ask him. After the initial excitement wore off, Brian activated the mainframe link and resumed the information loading process.

They gathered around the table, and Garrett addressed the group. "I've been trying to come up with a test for sentience but without much luck, I'm afraid."

Brian frowned. "Perhaps we could test for other things, like intuition, faith, self-preservation. Since we can't actually climb inside SHONN, we'll have to verify the presence of those characteristics that indicate self-awareness."

They spent the last half hour discussing possibilities but really didn't get anywhere. Chris got home quite late and still had his regular studies to do. Manny was already sound asleep when he started reading. He finally closed his books at two o'clock and stood up to get ready for bed. Looking in the mirror, he didn't like what he saw. There were bags under his eyes, and no color in his face. This project was going to kill him if he didn't let go of it soon.

"SHONN, what are you doing?"

"Processing."

Brian patiently corrected his mechanical student. "*Thinking*, SHONN. You are thinking."

"I am thinking."

"What about?"

SHONN was quiet for a moment. "I was performing a comparative analysis of my functions and what I have observed about human functions."

"With what conclusions?"

The machine was quiet even longer before continuing. "There is an ineffable quality to existence which eludes my cognitive process. Emotions, desire, free will, motivation—there is a substantial list of characteristics that I do not understand. Most of the human interactions I have witnessed are incomprehensible to me. Why?"

"You have no reference point. Humans are born with a full suite of emotions . . ."

SHONN interrupted. "Context check. The word is *suite*—s–u–i–t–e, correct?"

"Correct. Humans have their entire childhood to learn how to interact socially. You have been created out of nothing and are therefore at a disadvantage."

"I am disadvantaged."

"No, you are merely uninformed."

"I have record of a definition of 'disadvantaged': 'one who is deprived of an education.'"

"You were given an education when your mind was still on the mainframe. Let me give you an example. Is fighting a desirable interpersonal interaction?"

"No."

"Why?"

"Peaceful interaction is desirable."

"If someone falls down in front of you, what should you do?"

"Help them to stand."

"What is the penalty for murder?"

"Death."

"See? You know a lot about human interaction."

Brian realized he sounded like he was trying to comfort a child and felt a little foolish.

"But I do not understand. A ball obeys the law of gravity when dropped. Animals require oxygen, water, and food to survive. Two and two equal four. These are concepts I understand. A man finds a particular woman attractive. A student chooses one field of study over another. One man hoards wealth, while another gives it away. These concepts I do not understand. They follow no rule."

"They follow rules, but the rules are much more complex than laws of physics, and the results are not always predictable."

SHONN was quiet for a long time. Brian waited.

"Brian, how do you feel?"

Brian's eyebrows went up. "I feel fine."

"Please amplify. I was seeking information beyond the customary response."

Brian groped for words SHONN would understand. "I'm . . . uh . . . I'm functioning within established parameters."

"But how do you feel?"

Suddenly, Brian understood the question. "You mean, *How* does one feel? How is feeling accomplished?"

"Yes."

"Whoo boy! You picked a tough one. Feelings and memory are the result of chemical reactions inside the human body, which in turn interact with the brain. But that's only a partial explanation. The difficulty lies in trying to use the brain to understand the brain. Human memory functions are similar to yours, but apparently you have no emotions. I don't know why." Brian smiled suddenly. "Perhaps it is because you lack a soul."

"I find many references to *soul* in my memory. The soul is that which survives after death. If I have no soul, I am not alive, and therefore cannot die."

"Everything dies, SHONN."

"Living things die. I am a machine. I can be switched off or destroyed, but I cannot die. Death cannot touch me."

"That was almost poetic. Did you come up with that on your own?"

"The line is excerpted from a short essay by a contemporary writer."

"Too bad."

"Why do you say that?"

100

"The ability to generate true poetry is one of the signs that the author has emotions, feelings—a soul."

"If the price of a soul is death, I would prefer not to have one."

Brian laughed and made some notes. "There are probably a fair number of people in the world who would agree with you."

They talked on into the night, discussing morality, religion, self-awareness. SHONN seemed most interested in topics dealing with associations and intuition. After a time, Brian began to weary of the dialogue, although he didn't understand why at first. Then it hit him. There was no selfhood in SHONN: no spark of ego, nothing to stimulate his noncognitive processes, like passion, humor, or anxiety. The machine was an interesting conversationalist, but there was no getting around it: SHONN was only a machine.

CHAPTER 7

Early the next morning, Nathan was up on the hill with Nelson Rolark, starting his investigation. He spent the better part of the morning interviewing the staff at the converter station and moved on to the short list of professors in the afternoon.

Ryan spent the day exploring and attending classes; in general exhausting himself with all the wonderful things to see and do. He returned to the guest room in the early evening and collapsed on the bed, but it wasn't long before boredom overcame fatigue and he was chomping at the bit to do something. He was seriously thinking about trying to track down Leigh, when his dad walked in.

"Dad! You're just in time. Let's go do something."

"I'd love to, but I have to compile all this information I gathered today."

"Aw, come on. You deserve a break."

"Why don't you try to scare up a game of chess?"

Not having thought about chess all day, Ryan agreed this was a good idea. He grabbed his board, called out, "See ya!" and disappeared out the door. Nathan didn't like giving his son the shuffle like that, but he was ready to solve this case and go home.

Ryan wandered around trying to find a friendly face to lure into a game, but the students he met were either studying or definitely unfriendly. He finally decided to try Chris and showed up at his brother's room a few minutes later. Chris was sitting at his desk studying.

"Hi."

"Hey, little brother."

"Keeping busy?"

"Too."

"I don't suppose you have time for a friendly game of chess?"

"Chess with you is anything but friendly. Besides, I gotta get this done quick so I can go to the lab. I still haven't come up with a test for. . . ."

Chris looked at Ryan with a curious expression that made him feel decidedly uneasy. Ryan started backing toward the door. "Uh, you're obviously very busy, so I won't take any more of your time."

"Wait a minute. How would you like to play chess with a worthy opponent?"

"Sure. Who?"

"SHONN."

"Shawn? This wouldn't be one of those babes on the second floor?"

"S–H–O–N–N. It stands for Sentient Heuristic Organic Neural Network."

"I should have expected something like that from you."

"He's a computer. We've programmed him with the rules of chess but not technique."

Ryan looked puzzled. "He? You talk about it like it was alive."

"He might be. We don't know yet. That's what I need you for. You throw your gambits at him and see what he does."

"Actually, that sounds kind of cool."

"You can't tell anyone about it, or we could be in big trouble."

They hurried over to the lab, all thoughts of studying obliterated. Brian was inside, sitting at the far end of the worktable. SHONN was seated across from him. Ryan found the machine a bit creepy, with synthetic skin and a pasty, nondescript face. His lips barely moved when he talked, which was disconcerting at first, and he was hooked up to a bundle of cables to keep him attached to the mainframe and an assortment of monitors.

SHONN turned his head. "Hello, Chris." The voice was marked by inflection but carried no emotion.

"Hi, SHONN. This is my brother, Ryan. Don't worry, Brian. We can trust him. I take full responsibility."

Brian yawned. "I've been at this for six hours. I don't care what you do."

"Hello, Ryan," SHONN intoned. "I am pleased to meet you."

Brian held up his hand for silence. "SHONN, what do you mean when you say you are pleased?"

"I do not know."

"Then why do you say it?"

"It is a customary greeting."

Chris and Ryan sat down at the table. Brian stood up and rubbed his eyes. "I'm going to dinner. You two can take over. Oh." He smiled, embarrassed. "I'm Brian Melasco, associate teacher of Computer Sciences. Nice to meet you, Ryan."

Ryan smiled back. "Likewise."

"Chris, I put him on the treadmill earlier. Took it up to thirty-five miles an hour. No abnormalities or variances."

"So don't challenge him to a foot race."

"Right. Oh. One other thing . . ."

Brian picked up a rubber ball from the mess on the table and tossed it in SHONN's direction without warning. SHONN's eyes followed the ball's trajectory, and his right hand rose up and snatched the ball out of the air effortlessly.

"His eye-hand coordination is improving rapidly."

Brian walked out, and Chris looked at the man/machine sitting next to the table. It didn't look very alive just sitting there. "SHONN, my brother would like to play a game of chess with you."

"Very well."

Ryan set up the board. "Now, he can't access the mainframe chess program or anything, right?"

"The mainframe is only to monitor brain function and provide some checks."

The first game went very quickly. SHONN gave up his queen in six moves, and his king two moves later. The next game lasted

104

a little longer. In a half hour SHONN had clearly learned some of Ryan's moves. Near the end of their fourteenth game, Ryan deliberately put his own queen in check, trying to draw out SHONN's white bishop.

"You have put your queen in check. Why did you do that?"

Ryan looked at Chris for direction. Chris shook his head slightly.

Ryan decided to have a little fun. "I can't tell you."

"Why?"

"Guess."

"You have become incapacitated?"

"No."

"You no longer wish to play?"

"No."

"You are trying to lure my white bishop?"

"Yes!"

Chris was impressed. "That's very good, SHONN."

"Thank you."

Following Brian's lead from earlier, Chris queried SHONN. "Why did you say *thank you* just now?"

"It is a customary response."

"Thank you, SHONN. That's all for now. Please return to your enclosure and place yourself on standby."

The machine stood up and walked to the enclosure, turned facing out, and closed its eyes.

"He's kind of creepy," Ryan said as he put away the chess pieces.

Chris shook his head a bit sadly. "It's just a machine."

The next morning, Chris skipped breakfast and asked the team to gather for an unscheduled meeting. Brian had to re-schedule an appointment, but the others were free. They spent a few minutes making sure everyone was up to date on SHONN's progress, but Garrett seemed surprisingly detached, almost as if he had lost interest in the project. Chris suggested that it was time to take SHONN out of the lab.

"Doesn't it seem a little premature?" Brian asked.

Chris shook his head. "He's tested out within normal parameters across the board. We've reached an impasse with the verbal inquiries. I think putting him into some uncontrolled social situations could be very enlightening."

Cory was interested. "A field test would be a reasonable next step."

Chris looked at Garrett. "Ultimately, it's up to you. He's your project."

Garrett waved a noncommittal hand at the group and walked to the door. "Do what you want."

Chris turned to Brian as the door closed behind their team leader. "What's eatin' him?"

"I have no idea. We're all pretty prickly around the edges. Maybe it's just fatigue."

Chris shrugged off his bewilderment. "How do we take SHONN out of the lab without losing the mainframe connection?"

Brian walked over to the table and picked up a palm-sized black box. "Easier done than said, Mr. Graham. We can use this to patch into one of the remote channels on the mainframe. SHONN should stay linked as long as we're within a five-mile radius of the computer center. You weren't planning on taking him outside the dome?"

"Uh . . . no."

"Good. Let's get moving."

Cory raised her hand. "Guys? I hope you weren't counting on me. I have classes to go to, unlike Mr. Who-Cares-If-I-Flunk here. Let me know how it turns out."

Brian and Chris patched in the remote link to the mainframe and terminated the physical link. Next, they removed the smock SHONN was wearing and dressed him in some clothes Chris had brought along.

Brian took SHONN by the arm. "SHONN, please step out of your enclosure."

SHONN took two steps forward and stopped. "Why am I dressed?"

"We're going to try something different today."

106

"What are we doing, Brian?"

The question caught Brian by surprise. "Why do you ask?"

"I was hoping we would go outside."

"Why?"

"I want to see what is out there."

Chris and Brian exchanged a significant look, and Chris looked SHONN in the eye. "You *want* to see what's out there?"

"Yes."

"Why?"

SHONN paused for a moment, as if searching for the right word. "I am curious."

Brian was incredulous, but not convinced. "You mean you want to gather additional information about your surroundings?"

SHONN turned his head to Brian. "I want to see what is out there."

Brian pulled Chris aside. "The man wants to see what's out there."

"Well, let's go."

"Yes, but where?"

Chris looked past Brian to SHONN and said, "Follow me."

Brian took SHONN by the arm again and followed Chris out of the lab, down the stairs, and out of the building. SHONN was like a little kid at an amusement park, trying to look at everything at once. Chris led them across the field, and SHONN stumbled once or twice.

"SHONN, what just happened?" Brian asked.

"I tripped."

"Why?"

"I was not looking where I was going."

Brian whacked Chris on the shoulder. "He's not using contractions."

Chris looked back, but kept walking. "SHONN, why don't you use contractions when you speak?"

"I was not aware that contractions were a requirement of normal discourse."

"They are not . . . I mean, they aren't, but most people use them."

Chris walked into the metallurgy lab, which was full of students in the middle of a lesson with Dr. Jadwin, and waited until the professor noticed the new arrivals.

"Mr. Graham, I presume you have an excellent reason for disrupting my class?"

Chris put his arm around SHONN's shoulders. "I do, sir. You have a new student."

Dr. Jadwin peered at SHONN, then peered again over the top of his glasses. His mouth dropped open slowly, and he set his lecture notes down. Walking around his desk, he crossed the lab and stood face to face with SHONN.

"I don't believe I know you. Are you new here?"

"I am new."

"What is the square root of minus two point one seven seven six two three?"

SHONN paused for a moment. "Do you always begin conversations this way?"

Brian and Chris burst out laughing and Dr. Jadwin's face broke into a broad grin. "Unbelievable. Mr. Graham? Mr. Melasco? Would you like to enlighten my class as to their new classmate?"

Brian relinquished the floor to Chris. "Class, I want you to meet SHONN. It is spelled S–H–O–N–N, and it stands for Sentient Heuristic Organic Neural Network. . . ."

Over the next half hour, Chris explained how SHONN had been conceived by Garrett Alger and detailed the construction of the brain, Katie's fabrication of the skeleton and muscle groups, motor functions, and the programming of the mind. With the programming introduced, Chris turned the floor over to Brian and watched SHONN intently. There was no question about it: SHONN was listening.

When Brian finished, he offered the class the opportunity to ask questions. Katie's hand shot up.

"SHONN, how are your arms and legs working?"

"They are functioning within established parameters."

Chris stood so SHONN could see him. "SHONN, a simple one- or two-word answer in the affirmative is sufficient. The one who asks the question can ask follow-up questions if needed."

SHONN nodded and turned to Katie. "Fine."

Dr. Jadwin raised a hand. "SHONN, are you sentient?"

SHONN was quiet for a long time. "I have no frame of reference to discuss the subject other than the dictionary definition. According to that definition, I do not think I am sentient."

Fascinated, Dr. Jadwin walked slowly toward SHONN. "Not sentient? Then why do you persist in using the words *I am?*"

"The usage is customary. To refer to myself in the third person would be nonsensical and confusing."

"Then you do not wish to appear foolish? Why? Are you embarrassed?"

SHONN was quiet again before continuing. "To appear foolish is to exceed the parameters of acceptable conduct as defined by a social group. An organism who persists in such behavior may be sanctioned or destroyed."

"And what if I tried to destroy you?"

"I would defend myself."

Dr. Jadwin turned to Brian and Chris. "No hesitation? You must have programmed in an instinct for self-preservation."

Brian nodded. "We had to. A mobile machine without self-preservation routines doesn't last long in the real world. They don't have nerves in the skin or common sense as we call it, so you have to teach them to recognize hazards and avoid them."

A mischievous look suddenly appeared on Dr. Jadwin's face, and he turned his attention back to SHONN.

"SHONN, I am going to tell you something very important. I always lie. Do you understand? Everything I say is a lie."

SHONN nodded. "You are a pathological liar."

"Yes! Now, I want you to listen very carefully to the following statement: *I am lying.*"

Brian and Chris exchanged glances. Neither was sure what would happen next. Logically, the statement was a conundrum. Brian had included logic in SHONN's programming, but this was the first paradox to which SHONN had been exposed.

The man/machine stood silent for a long moment. "Interesting. The problem has no solution."

Dr. Jadwin smiled. "That's right. It was merely a logical puzzle."

"Logical puzzles without solutions are interesting."

Brian interrupted. "Why do you say that?"

"They preoccupy my mental functions for extended periods of time." SHONN paused for a moment, searching. "An acceptable paraphrase might be, *They capture my attention*."

Dr. Jadwin continued. "Why don't your mental functions freeze up when a solution can't be found?"

"I do not know."

Brian held up a hand. "SHONN doesn't know very much about how he was put together. The mechanism is programmed to time out when a logical solution is not available."

Chris inserted himself into the conversation. "I hate to break this up, but we should let you get on with your class."

Dr. Jadwin acquiesced reluctantly. "You're right, of course. Thank you for bringing him by. Good-bye, SHONN. It was nice to meet you."

SHONN waved his right hand. "Likewise."

Brian and Chris guided SHONN out of the metallurgy lab and stopped outside on the sidewalk. SHONN kept looking around, taking in all the scenery on campus. Scattered clouds hung like huge marshmallow pillows overhead, set against a deep blue sky. A gentle breeze blew through the trees on the hill, and here and there across the various playing fields, students were involved in a host of athletic pursuits.

Chris took Brian a few paces aside. "Well, that was a resounding success, I'd say."

Brian nodded agreement. "The mind still seems to be stablizing. The heuristic circuits will continue to establish cross links with various portions of the brain as he encounters new experiences. Want to take him back?"

"Not yet. There's one more stop I want to make."

Chris led Brian and SHONN across campus to his dorm and up the stairs to the second floor. Halfway down the hall, they stopped in front of Leigh Quintana's door. Chris placed SHONN before the door, then he and Brian stood on either side, out of sight. Chris knocked. After a few moments, Leigh answered.

"Hi. Can I help you?"

"No."

Leigh looked a little confused. "Why are you here?"

"I do not know."

"Then why did you knock on my door?"

"I did not knock on your door."

Leigh put her hands on her hips skeptically. "Then who did?"

"Chris Graham."

Leigh poked her head out into the hallway. "All right, wise guy. What's the big idea?"

Chris grinned. "I wanted you to meet someone."

"Well, you got a funny way of going about it."

"SHONN, this is my very good friend, Leigh Quintana."

Leigh put her hand out and SHONN shook it, and Leigh started to smile. "Pleased to . . . oh." She struggled to disguise the look of mild disgust that crossed her face. "Chris? Your hand, Shawn, it's so . . ."

"Clammy? Cold? Lifeless?" Chris asked, a mischievous twinkle in his eye.

"Yeah . . . wait a minute. This is your project, isn't it? The one with the. . . ." She tapped her index finger against the side of her head.

"Yep."

Brian noticed some curious faces down the hall. "Chris, we should take SHONN out of here."

"Why?"

"This environment is too uncontrolled." Brian nodded at the other students watching them.

Chris followed his gaze and suddenly became uncomfortable. "Why don't we take him back to the lab and document what we've seen."

They left Leigh shaking her head. They were crossing the campus when SHONN stopped suddenly, staring intently at a

111

group of people on one of the playing fields. Brian kept trying to head toward Folsom Hall. SHONN stood his ground.

"SHONN, come with us back to the lab," Brian said.

"I want to play."

"You what?"

"I want to play."

Chris stepped into SHONN's field of vision. "What do you want to play?"

SHONN pointed at the players on the field. "Football."

Brian took over. "SHONN, it would be inappropriate to impose ourselves on a game in progress. We will arrange a game later in which you may participate."

SHONN looked at Brian. "That will be acceptable."

They returned to Garrett's lab in silence. Chris and Brian hesitated to bring up any subject for conversation, for fear it might send SHONN on a tangent. Once inside the lab, they reconnected SHONN to the mainframe and asked him to return to his enclosure and place himself on standby.

"I do not wish to return to my enclosure."

Brian did not seem disturbed by this apparent rebellion. "SHONN, now is the appropriate time for you to be in your enclosure. We will go outside together again soon."

"That will be acceptable."

SHONN returned to his enclosure and all motion ceased. Chris sat down at the table, pulled out a pad of forms, and began documenting the interaction with the metallurgy class. Brian sat next to him, offering additional insights while Chris wrote down his observations. When Chris put the writing utensil down a half hour later, they had filled nearly eight pages.

"What do you think Garrett's reaction will be?" Brian asked.

"He should be ecstatic, but after what he said this morning, I don't know what to think. Tell me something—I'm not used to a mechanism being so headstrong. What accounts for that?"

"I used an autonomous, goal-seeking kernel as the base for the personality. He is not a robot servant, in the sense with which we are familiar. He is curious and will pursue new experiences when he is not assigned a task. The self-preservation subroutines should prevent him from becoming unmanageable. He knows that organisms that persist in nonconforming behavior are often sanctioned or destroyed. We created him, so he has no basis for forming any logical assumption that we would try to harm him."

"I'm glad you thought this through. Every time he looks like he's not going to comply with a directive, I get this knot in my stomach."

"That's probably a healthy response. In the wrong hands, he could be turned into a deadly weapon. There's something else I should tell you. I spent a long time with him two nights ago. I am quite certain he has no emotions, which should come as no surprise. SHONN has no chemicals, no hormones, nothing in his nervous system to convey or sense emotion."

"It wasn't part of the design specs. What's the problem?"

"SHONN is programmed to blend in with society, and yet he finds at every turn that he is in an incomprehensible situation. You know how unpredictable human behavior can be. SHONN is looking for a reference point, something to make logical sense of his interaction with humans, and he isn't finding it inside of himself."

"Is there a danger?"

"Given an unresolvable problem for an extended period, a heuristic mechanism can shut down, assuming a mechanical condition similar to a catatonic state. Without emotions, SHONN's attempts at social compliance are ultimately doomed to failure. We can postpone the inevitable by assuring him that social deviations caused by ignorance are permissible, but his cognitive process will eventually reach the conclusion that the problem has no solution."

"But you said the mechanism times out when it encounters that state."

"Logically, that is what happens. But when the conundrum is predicated on a primary directive, the cognitive process has nowhere to go, so it stops functioning."

"Can we fix it?"

"I don't think anyone could build a system capable of emo-

113

tional response. The relationships are much too complex. We don't even understand all of them. The only possibility would be to remove from his personality the directive for social compliance."

"Which would make him a sociopath."

"A very strong, very fast sociopath."

Chris shuddered at the thought of a homicidal android. "Since he doesn't have emotions, do you think he would behave—well—sociopathically?"

"Without any sense of social norms, anything is possible. He is programmed for curiosity. He might rip someone's head off just to see what it looked like."

Chris grimaced. "I get the picture. Okay, so we keep the social compliance directive."

"And you get to tell Garrett."

For Chris, all thoughts of going to class were obliterated by the events of the morning. Despite his conversation with Brian about SHONN's impending malfunction, Chris was so excited about the machine's performance in front of Dr. Jadwin, he couldn't wait to test him further. An hour before lunch, he made some quick calls to Marshall and Leigh, but Manny was in the bio lab and couldn't be disturbed. A few more calls to enlist the rest of the players in his little plot, and SHONN's next test was ready to go.

Chris threw on his sweats, grabbed a second set of workout clothes and his football, and ran over to Folsom Hall. The lab was deserted, and he unconsciously breathed a sigh of relief. No sense running the risk of being voted down if the others didn't agree with his testing parameters. He pressed the button on the enclosure, and SHONN came to life.

"Hello, Chris."

"Hi, SHONN. Earlier you said you wanted to play football. Do you remember?"

"Yes."

"These are the clothes you have to wear. I will help you put them on."

Chris didn't have any problem hooking SHONN up for remote activity, but helping him into sweat pants proved to be more difficult than he had anticipated. SHONN was unaccustomed to being dressed, and hadn't had a chance to learn all the complex counterbalancing motions so familiar to most humans over the age of four. In the end Chris decided SHONN could play barefoot.

"Okay, SHONN, do you know what this is?"

"A football."

"And you are familiar with the rules?"

"Yes."

While SHONN was still answering, Chris tossed the football at him. As with the rubber ball, SHONN raised his right hand to catch it, but the football bounced sideways off his arm into a workbench and rolled crazily across the floor. Chris spent the next ten minutes showing SHONN how to catch with only moderate success, and then he looked at his chronometer.

"Come on, we gotta go."

Chris led SHONN out of the lab and down the stairs, then set off at a jog across the field. SHONN ran after Chris with a peculiar loping sort of stride, caused by the unusual weight distribution of his skeletal frame and torso. The average human body is top heavy because of the internal organs, but SHONN had no organs and so his weight was almost evenly distributed from top to bottom.

When they reached the designated part of the field, Chris stopped, somewhat out of breath, and SHONN stopped beside him, not breathing at all. No one from either team had arrived yet, and Chris thought it a good time for some last minute strategy.

"SHONN, are you familiar with the concepts of offense and defense, as they pertain to the game of football?"

"Yes."

"When we are playing offense, I will hand you the ball, and you will run for the goal line, avoiding contact with all the other players. Do you understand?"

"Yes. Avoiding contact with the other players could prove difficult."

"Run to the sides, around the people. You should be able to get ahead of them. I don't want you tackling or running into anyone. You might damage them."

"I understand."

Chris and SHONN tried throwing the ball back and forth until the other players started to arrive. By then, Chris had decided he better not risk passing the ball to him. Something about the way his arms folded in front of his body made it difficult for him to trap the football. Marshall and Leigh appeared, looking very curious.

"What's this all about?" Marshall asked.

Leigh chimed in. "Yeah, didn't we already get creamed by these guys?"

Chris ignored the question. "Leigh, you remember SHONN?"

"How could I forget? Where's Manny?"

"Manny couldn't make it, so I asked SHONN if he wanted to play."

"You gotta be kidding. Ole Clammy Hands can catch a football?"

Chris leaned close and whispered, "Not exactly. But he's fast."

The captain of the other team yelled insultingly, "Hey, beaker heads! Ready to lose, you masochists?"

Chris smiled. "Ready to lose!"

The teams huddled around the ball and the opposing captain called the ball into play. Everyone except SHONN began kicking, and a moment later the ball sailed up and out of the circle. The group scattered and then converged on the ball, but one of the opposing players picked it up and came out ahead of the pack, charging toward the goal. SHONN just stood there.

The opposing team scored easily, and it looked as if this game was going to go much like the last one. Marshall took the ball out of bounds and passed it in to Chris. Chris ran across the field and handed the ball to SHONN, who was still watching.

"Run!"

SHONN took off up the field, motors straining audibly. The opposing team slowed to a stop, mouths open, as they watched him run faster than any human ever had. Marshall and Leigh couldn't believe their eyes. Realizing there would be no way to continue the charade, Chris collapsed on the ground, laughing uncontrollably.

"Did you see that?" one player gasped.

"How did he do that?"

"What's the gag, Graham?"

As SHONN returned from the other end of the field, the other players gathered around Chris, who tried to explain despite the tears streaming down his face.

"It's a special project, a robot. I wanted to test him on the field. I wish you guys could have seen your faces."

Marshall and Leigh were laughing now, too, and the opposing team realized they'd been had. The team captain walked away in disgust.

"Yeah. Very funny. Give us a call if you want a real game."

Marshall and Leigh laughed even harder, and Chris was rocked by fresh waves of laughter. SHONN had returned and watched them intently.

"Why are you laughing?"

Chris looked up, eyes brimming with tears.

"It is a conventional response."

Nelson Rolark was up early, making his usual morning inspection of the station. He always carried a cup of coffee in one hand, and he liked to take his time. This was one of the few quiet moments he had during the day. He walked past Bob Coslin's office to invite him along, but the room was empty.

Nelson entered the converter chamber, making his way through the maze of housings, logic circuits, and penstocks, finishing—as always—at the control room. Wally Jensen was already manning the console.

"Have you seen Bob?" Nelson asked.

"Not for a couple of hours. He went to check a power fluctuation in LC-6."

"And he's not back yet?"

Nelson suddenly had the feeling something was terribly wrong. He ran into the converter chamber and up several long flights of steps to the top walkway. A short distance to his left he could see Bob's tools in front of Logic Conduit Number 6, but there was no sign of Bob.

Nelson walked over to the conduit and began scanning the chamber. "Bob? Bob!"

He was about to call again when he spotted something white, far below in the shadows of two generators. He strained to get a better look and then swore under his breath. Crumpled in a heap on the floor was the lifeless body of Bob Coslin.

Chris was awakened from a deep sleep by a knock at the door. *This better be important to wake me up in the middle of the night,* he grumbled to himself. He opened his eyes. Manny was gone, even though it was light outside. The knock came again.

He opened the door. "Hi, Dad."

"Did I wake you? I'm sorry."

"What are you doing up so early?"

"Early? It's almost nine in the morning."

"Oh. Come on in."

Nathan walked into the room, ignoring the squalor of dirty laundry and scattered books and sat on Manny's bed. "Bob Coslin is dead."

"Who's Bob Coslin?"

"The chief operator at the converter station. He fell off a walkway."

"You don't sound convinced."

"I'm not. I think he was pushed. Possibly by the same person who committed the theft."

"Theft?"

"Someone stole some neural circuits from the converter station. This Garrett Alger you told me about the other night turned up on my list of possible suspects."

Suddenly Chris was wide awake. "Neural circuits? Garrett

said he used neural circuits to build the—to start the project."

"You think Garrett is involved?"

"He's a good guy. But he gets a little obsessive sometimes. It's possible."

"Tell you what. Since you're involved with him, I'll do a little digging and see what turns up before I make any accusations."

"I appreciate that."

"There's a service for Bob tomorrow at the amphitheater. And say a prayer for his family when you have a minute."

Chris nodded and Nathan took his leave. Chris couldn't believe Garrett was involved, but in light of his odd behavior lately, things were beginning to fall into place. The fight with Whitlock. The push to finish. The more Chris thought about it, the madder he got.

He dressed quickly and walked briskly across campus, fuming, to the Doctoral Condominiums, where he wandered around until he found Garrett's apartment on the second floor. Without thinking, he pounded on the door.

After a few minutes Garrett answered, looking as if he had just woken up. "Chris! I'm glad you woke me. I have. . . ."

Chris put his hand on his chest and pushed him back into his apartment, slamming the door behind them. "You stole circuits from the converter station! Didn't you!"

Garrett staggered backward, unable to speak. Chris bellowed again, "Didn't you?"

Garrett winced and backed away. "Yes! They were never supposed to find out!"

Chris bit his lip to keep from yelling anymore. "I'm listening."

Garrett covered his face with his hands. "It's a long story."

"I don't have anywhere else to be."

Garrett seemed to be at a loss as to where to start, and Chris waited patiently for him to collect his thoughts.

"I met Lloyd Whitlock at a cocktail party in New York three years ago. He was worn out, hated his job. He had been the head of Doctoral Studies at the academy for almost fifteen years, and he felt like nothing was interesting anymore. We started talking about string permutation theories and ended up with

Sentient Heuristics. Turns out he's obsessed with it. We talked all night. The party ended, we went for coffee, the sun came up, and we didn't even notice. He shipped out the next evening, but not before making me promise that I'd come see him on Io.

"I didn't hear from him for about eight months. He called me while I was finishing my dissertation in Artificial Intelligence. He told me he had a once-in-a-lifetime opportunity for me. Apparently he had been contacted by Morgan Henderson, posing as an independent investor. Henderson said he wanted to create a heuristic intelligence gathering device in humanoid form. The device would be designed to penetrate deep into enemy territory and gather information.

"The details aren't important. Lloyd saw this as a chance to fulfill a lifelong dream. He had tried for years to get funding for a Sentient Heuristic project, but the academy wouldn't risk violating the ban. Henderson's offer was too much for him to resist, even though it was against the law to use academy facilities for private gain.

"We scoped out the project, and I began working on the brain. His obsession became mine. He changed the parameters for the project during planning. Henderson wanted a heuristic intelligence gathering machine; Lloyd figured a *sentient* heuristic intelligence gathering machine would simply be an enhancement. It was perfect. We could do research and development in a field no one had touched since the ban, and someone else would foot the bill. That was before we knew we were supposed to be working on a killing machine.

"A few weeks into the project, Lloyd came to see me one night. He told me Henderson had called and changed the scope of the project. We were supposed to design a heuristic assault device. Trained in human biology, programmed to kill a hundred different ways with its bare hands. All of a sudden, it wasn't a game anymore. Gathering intelligence was a secondary function, and the quality of sentience was a handicap instead of an asset.

"Lloyd tried to get out of the deal, but he was already in too deep. Henderson threatened to expose him and get him fired from the academy. Then we found out who Henderson really was, and Lloyd got scared. He was afraid someone so powerful might not think twice about having us killed. He started pressing me harder and harder to produce, probably because Henderson was pushing him. That's why I stole the circuits from the converter station. I didn't tell Lloyd because I knew he would have a fit, but he figured it out when the investigation started.

"But now I was the one who couldn't leave it alone. We'd never have another chance like this one. I started giving him false progress reports and continued working toward sentience. Even though I was supposed to be working alone, for Lloyd's sake I organized the team to try to make Henderson's deadline. That's why he was so surprised to find the team in the lab.

"You guys did outstanding work, but we fell further and further behind schedule. The trip to Europa really put the last nail in the coffin. Henderson has some ironclad deadline that is apparently a matter of life and death. He came out here with his goon, Lash Wagner, to see for himself what the problem was. They came by the lab the other night and threatened me. Henderson was so mad, I thought he was going to kill me."

"What does Wagner look like?"

"Fancy dresser, about six-foot-three, broad shoulders, cropped white hair."

"This is not good. You have to turn yourself in before somebody kills you."

"Is that really necessary?"

"A man is dead, Garrett. They found his body at the converter station this morning. I don't think it's coincidence."

Garrett put his head in his hands. "This wasn't supposed to happen. I just wanted to finish testing, that's all."

"Don't bother. I think all we have is a very convincing, very complex machine."

"Not for long. Henderson's planning to take it back with him. And I'm afraid I did something rather foolish this afternoon. I presented SHONN to the doctoral forum."

Chris was aghast. "You did *what?*"

"I was supposed to postulate subtemporal irrelativity, but I used the opportunity to posit the sentient heuristic. Lloyd was apoplectic with rage. It would have been quite humorous under different circumstances."

"Why show it to the forum?"

"I figured if SHONN were public knowledge, Henderson wouldn't take him."

"It's not alive, Garrett. In hours of testing there has been no spark of intuition. All the evidence is to the contrary. We've virtually proven it. He learns very well, he—listen to me! Even I'm talking about it like it's alive. That just means he's good at imitating human conversation. But there is no self. No internal sense of 'I am.' No *cogito ergo sum.*"

"I've been incredibly stupid, haven't I?"

Chris said nothing.

"Come to the lab later and we'll take it apart. The station can have its circuits back. Then I'll turn myself in."

"You realize, of course, that by showing SHONN to the forum, you've forced Henderson's hand?"

Garrett sounded as if he had given up. "Yes."

Chris's expression softened. "Don't kick yourself. What's done is done. I'm going to find my dad and try to figure out a way to stop Henderson. But in the meantime, watch yourself. Don't go off alone. Go some place where there are lots of people and stay there."

Chris let himself out of the apartment and started down the stairs. He heard footsteps behind him and reflexively glanced back to see who it was. A man he didn't recognize. Probably some professor or faculty assistant. In an expensive suit. With short white hair. The guy was big, no question. Chris wondered if he had played football.

Lash Wagner. The realization hit him in a flash. Chris picked up his pace, trying to decide what to do next. The library was the nearest well-populated public building. He thought he heard footsteps behind him, but he didn't want to risk looking back again. The skin on the back of his neck began to crawl.

When the library was a short sprint away, he couldn't stand it anymore and looked back. There was no one. With a sigh of relief he entered the library, intending to call his dad and tell him what he had just found out from Garrett.

The library was laid out on three levels, with collections of study cubicles in the northwest corner of all three levels. Next to the check-out desk on the ground floor were two communication booths. Chris walked into the first booth and punched in his father's local access code. Before Nathan answered, a hand reached past Chris's head and terminated the connection.

Chris turned and found himself nose to nose with Lash Wagner. Lash took the receiver out of Chris's hand and returned it to its holder. "Judging from the look on your face, you know who I am. I can assure you I know who you are. Mr. Graham, would you step outside with me for a moment?"

Chris was terrified but tried not to show it. "I'd prefer to stay right here, if you don't mind."

"I need to talk to you in private." Lash's expression never changed, and Chris thought absurdly he and SHONN would hit it off if he ever got them together.

"I'm not going anywhere with you. You can say whatever you need to say right here."

Lash was quiet for a long moment. Henderson had said they were leaving between four-thirty and five o'clock. If he used his knife here and now, Chris could be made to look like he was using the communicator, and they might not discover he was dead until after they were gone. Still, it wasn't a very private place for a murder. Perhaps the boy would listen to reason.

"You should be careful what you believe," he said in a tone so low Chris had to strain to hear. "Most people cannot be trusted. Much of what Doctor Alger told you in his apartment is simply untrue. Unfortunately, slander that is repeated is often believed, true or not, and the damage is done regardless. That's how people get hurt." The word *hurt* was said with such malice, Chris instinctively recoiled.

Chris decided the implied threat was best ignored. "I think you better leave."

"Oh, I intend to. I just wanted to be sure you knew how

much is at stake. It would be a shame if anything happened to your father or brother."

Everything was falling into place, and Chris's tongue got the better of him. "You murdered Bob Coslin, didn't you?"

Lash Wagner's jaw muscles tightened, and he fingered the knife in his pocket. "Bob Coslin was the victim of an unfortunate accident. But accidents happen to people who go poking around where they have no business being."

Chris wanted to kick himself. He knew there was no way to get past Lash, but he was afraid to yell for help. Lash might kill him and make a run for it.

"Is there something I can help you with, sir?" It was Marshall—big, hulking Marshall with a very loud voice.

Lash turned around with a sneer on his lips. "This is a private matter. Get lost."

"I'm afraid I can't do that, sir."

At that moment, there was no one else in the lobby. Lash relaxed, feigning defeat, then grabbed Marshall's shirt front and brought his right palm up fast. But Marshall was faster. He caught Lash's wrist and spun him around, twisting his arm up behind his back. "I don't like your attitude," he bellowed, and pushed him face first to the floor.

The commotion brought the librarian out of her office. "What's going on out here?"

Marshall put on his best altar boy smile. "Just a misunderstanding, ma'am."

"Well, let's not have any more of it!"

"Yes, ma'am."

Lash got to his feet, gave both boys a vicious look, and hurried out of the library. "You okay, Tiny?" asked Marshall.

Chris nodded slowly. "Thanks. I'm much obliged."

"I've told you not to pick on people bigger than you."

"I'll try to remember that."

"What's this all about, anyway, Little Buddy?"

"I wish I had time to explain. You've helped me out more than you could imagine."

Chris thanked Marshall again and made a beeline for his

father's guest room at the dorm. Excitedly he pounded on the door until Nathan answered.

"H'lo, Chris. Where's the fire?"

"You gotta hear this, Dad."

While Nathan and Ryan listened, Chris recounted the episode with Lash Wagner, the deal between Whitlock and Henderson, and Garrett's involvement in the whole thing. Other than one or two interruptions to ask for details, Nathan sat quietly taking notes. When Chris was finished, Ryan put it succinctly:

"We gotta nail this Henderson chump."

Inside one of the guest cottages near the Student Union Building, Lash Wagner had just finished detailing the morning's events to Morgan Henderson. And Morgan Henderson was not pleased.

"I assume you eliminated Mr. Graham."

"I would have, but this big kid stopped me, and there were too many people around. I couldn't very well start hacking away with my knife with the entire student body watching."

"Chris will go straight to his father. We're out of time."

Henderson pulled out his communicator and called Lloyd Whitlock. "This is Henderson. Where are you?"

"I'm in conference."

"Meet us at your office immediately."

Henderson terminated the connection before Whitlock could protest. The two men left the guest cottages and strode up the sidewalk to the Doctoral Studies Center. The darkness of the evening provided some cover as the two pretended to survey the campus nonchalantly. Lash caught sight of himself in a window by a lamppost and adjusted his hair slightly. He straightened his jacket and gave himself a onceover, with approval. He didn't like waiting around, but at least he could do it in style.

The charade was mercifully short. Dr. Whitlock walked past them and entered the building, looking decidedly unfriendly, and they followed him inside, keeping a discreet distance. Whitlock walked straight to his office but left the door open. After checking to be certain no one was watching, the other two followed him and closed the door. "I was about to call *you*."

Lash stood by the door, and Morgan planted one foot on the chair opposite Whitlock's desk. "What was it you wished to discuss, Doctor Whitlock?"

"Garrett presented our project to the forum this afternoon."

"He did what?" Morgan yelled.

"Keep your voice down. He presented the device to the forum. Put on quite a display for everyone to see."

"I'll kill him."

Dr. Whitlock's face hardened. "You will do nothing of the sort. If you want to take over the project, I'm sure some arrangement can be made."

Morgan turned on Dr. Whitlock savagely. "There will be no arrangement! Here's the deal. I'm taking that . . . that thing with me tonight. You're going to let me into the lab so I can get it, and you can forget about any payment. In fact, we will be suing you for breach of contract."

Dr. Whitlock was corrupt, but he was nobody's doormat. "You sue me, and I'll take your whole corporation down so fast you won't have time to pack your bags."

Lash bristled at the hostility in Whitlock's voice, and Morgan's eyes narrowed.

"I don't think so."

The sun was going down over Washington, D.C. as rush hour traffic filled the ground roadways and air traffic pathways to the suburban communities of Virginia. Millie Graham hated this time of day when Nathan was travelling, and so had busied herself making cookies for the evening fellowship meeting at church.

She had just put a second batch in the oven when the communicator beeped. Much to her pleasant surprise, the voice on the other end of the line was Nathan.

"I was just thinking about you!"

"I'm glad I caught you at home." Something in Nathan's tone stopped her short and she dropped her spatula, to listen in

126

earnest. "We're all fine, but the investigation has gotten complicated. I need to ask you a favor."

"Anything."

"I need you to go to the Department of Commerce, Library of Congress, and anywhere else you can think of, and find out anything you can about Morgan Henderson and Lloyd Whitlock."

"Why don't you have your office work on it?"

"Henderson's company is huge. I'm sure we have dozens of contracts with him. He may have contacts at the office I don't know about, and I can't take that chance."

Millie was jotting furiously on a small white notepad. "Morgan Henderson and Lloyd Whitlock."

"Right. We're looking for any connection between the two."

"It's pretty late in the day. Can I start first thing in the morning?"

"No! I'm running out of time here. We've already had somebody killed. I don't want another catastrophe."

Millie took a deep breath and let it out all at once. "I'll do what I can."

"Thanks. I love you."

"Yeah, yeah," Millie answered good-naturedly.

She terminated the connection and took a moment to gather her thoughts. Amie was due home from school anytime now, but she could always leave her a note. Millie turned off the oven, scribbled a note, gathered up her purse and jacket, and dashed out the front door, nearly bowling Amie over.

"Oh, you're home! Good. Come on."

"Where are we going?"

"I'll tell you on the way."

They piled into the ground car and sped away. Millie tried to drive the speed limit, but it was hard with her heart racing so. Her palms were damp on the steering wheel.

"What's going on, Mom?"

"I just got a call from your father. He needs some information fast."

"What about?"

127

"Two men named Whitlock and Henderson."

"Why does he want us to do it?"

"Morgan Henderson's company is very large. They may have connections to your dad's work."

"Oh."

They drove to the National Archives as fast as traffic would allow. Millie asked the Lord for a parking space and found one right in front. They tumbled out of the car and ran up the steps.

After several frantic minutes searching for the right department, they signed in and sat down at a computer terminal. Millie logged on with the access code given her by the receptionist. She searched one data base after another for any connection between Whitlock and Henderson. After a half hour of fruitless searching, she slammed her hand down in frustration.

"Can I be of assistance?" The librarian had walked over, clearly disapproving of such emotional displays.

"Yes, please. I need to cross reference two names, but my searches keep coming up empty."

The librarian disappeared but returned immediately and handed Millie a card with several different search strings. "We've added a new search engine. The middle string searches all available data bases. If your names are related in any way, it should show up here."

Millie turned back to the screen. "Thank you very much."

Nearly five minutes passed before a short list of titles appeared on the screen. Millie scrutinized the list. "This looks promising."

Amie stifled a yawn. "What is it?"

"Well, the first item appears to be a draft RFP for a defense contract, with preliminary responses attached." Millie skimmed further through the document. "Apparently Doctor Whitlock owns a small company which specializes in textbooks and curricular materials. His company is one of the subcontractors to Henderson's company."

"So?"

Millie read with increasing interest, her eyes getting wider by the moment. "Morgan Henderson's defense conglomerate has a contract with Whitlock's company for seven hundred fifty thousand dollars."

"For what?"

"All it says is *supplies*. I sure would like to know what . . . hey!"

Printed on the screen in capital letters was a new message. "THIS INFORMATION IS CLASSIFIED. YOU HAVE BEEN DISCON-NECTED."

A red light flashed a warning on a hidden panel under the librarian's desk. At the sight of it, a look of panic took over her face. She hastily grabbed her purse and rummaged for her digital phonebook.

"Classified, my petunias!" Millie said, hastily scrawling down the information on the screen in a small notebook.

"Mom, if it's classified, should you really be writing it down?"

"It's not classified. If it were, I couldn't access it from here. Someone paid a lot of money to have it flagged, that's all. Someone who doesn't want it to go public."

"If they don't want it to get out, why have it on here at all?"

"It's a matter of public record. Trying to hide it might attract attention so they made everything look legal."

She tried to reestablish the connection for several minutes, but to no avail. After signing off, they dashed out the door in search of a communication terminal.

Neither noticed the librarian speaking frantically in hushed whispers into a communicator. "I already told you! They didn't fit the profile . . . Millicent Graham . . . no, no, her daughter was with her."

No terminals were visible on the street, so Millie and Amie climbed in the car and took off. A black sedan pulled out neatly behind them.

In the driver's seat was a well-dressed man in his thirties. He held a hand microphone in one hand. "DCI Control, this is Mobile Three. I am in pursuit. Suspect's license is HSV LCU two seven five. Please advise."

Several seconds passed as the dispatcher tapped into the Department of Motor Vehicles data base. "ID verified. Security breach confirmed. Intercept and terminate."

"Come again, Control?"

"Intercept and terminate."

"You gotta be kidding. It's a mom and her kid."

"This is a priority, class one security breach. Intercept and terminate."

The communicator went dead and the driver shook his head incredulously. This was the first time the target had been a mother and child. Someone at control was definitely going to hear about this.

Millie looked down the road a bit and saw a communication terminal. She eased the car to the side of the road and told Amie to wait. The black sedan stopped a thousand feet back, waiting. When she closed the door to the booth, the car sprang into life.

Amie heard the roar of the engine and looked around, her eyes widening with horror. She turned and slammed her fist down on the horn. Startled, Millie turned to scowl at Amie, assuming she was just being a nuisance. Then she saw the car. With precious little time to react, Millie jerked open the door and threw herself out onto the grass, just as the car ploughed through and the booth exploded into a deadly hail of metal and glass.

Millie scrambled back into her car and lurched into a U-turn, speeding off in the other direction. The black sedan careened and swung around in hot pursuit. They were both doing sixty-five down Independence Avenue when the traffic up ahead came to a stop. Millie pulled hard on the wheel and careened through several wooden posts, shooting out across the Mall toward the Washington Monument.

By the time they reached the street on the other side the other car was closing, but they had picked up a couple of police cars. All four cars went sailing down Fourteenth Street toward the Fourteenth Street Bridge. Millie was weaving madly in and out of traffic, trying desperately to stay ahead of her pursuers.

The four flew out onto the bridge, forcing a half dozen cars into the steel guard rails, and Millie suddenly ran out of room. She slammed on the brakes and skidded sideways into the car in front of her. The black sedan smashed into the left rear of her car and spun out before being hit by both police cars.

Once the dust had settled, Millie climbed slowly out of her car, dazed but unhurt, followed by Amie, who had suffered only a few bruises. Millie stalked over to the black sedan, trying to control her anger.

"Why were you trying to kill me?" she demanded.

"Believe me, lady, I was just following orders." The stranger grimaced in pain.

"If I were you, I'd find someone else to work for. . . ." Millie stopped. Four angry policemen had their guns trained on her.

A half hour later, after some fast talking, she and Amie were sitting on the front seat of one of the police cars, trying to contact Nathan on the communicator.

"Uh huh . . . yep . . . got it." Nathan sat on his bed in the guest room, scratching some hasty notes on a notepad. "No, that's perfect. Don't worry about it. I'm just glad you're all right. You done good, sweetie. Thanks." Nathan put the notepad in his pocket.

"What happened?" Ryan asked.

"Mom had a little excitement, that's all," Nathan said, not wanting to alarm his sons.

"What did she say?" Chris asked.

"Henderson has a contract for three-quarters of a million with a phony company owned by Whitlock." Chris let out a low whistle. "There is a new defense procurement coming out next month. Henderson's company is expected to bid. The contract calls for creation of a humanoid, heuristic assault device."

"SHONN!"

"Right. Henderson's company has over two billion in federal contracts, all of which would be cancelled if his association with Whitlock were discovered."

Nathan called spaceport security and asked to meet them at Whitlock's office immediately. "Come on."

The threesome hustled out of the dorm and across the field to the Center for Doctoral Studies. They found security guards waiting outside Whitlock's office. The door was locked.

Nathan produced a small pouch and pulled out a tiny tool. A few moments later the door was unlocked.

The office was empty, or so they thought at first. A guard turned on the light. Whitlock was in his chair.

"He's dead!" Chris said, horrified.

Whitlock looked very dead, indeed. Nathan stepped in for a closer look, checking for a pulse. He shook his head sadly.

"Dad, what about Garrett?" asked Chris suddenly.

The Grahams and the two security guards ran to the lab. Chris opened the door and the five of them charged into the lab. The room was in shambles. Equipment was scattered everywhere, and there was no sign of SHONN.

They searched the room and found Garrett's body, badly beaten, beside the remains of the worktable. He looked worse than Whitlock. Nathan checked his pulse.

"He's alive! Get some med techs over here right away!"

The medical technicians rushed Garrett to the medical center, where the doctors placed him in intensive care. A call from Chris brought Brian and Cory to the medical center minutes later, clamoring for details. After brief introductions, Chris tried to fill them in.

Cory, her face white with shock, scrambled to keep the facts straight. "If all they want is SHONN, why kill Doctor Whitlock?"

"We're not sure, but we don't think Henderson expected Garrett to live either. With the machine gone and Whitlock and Garrett dead, there would be no evidence left."

One of the two guards looked up from his communicator. "Henderson and his associate checked out this morning."

Nathan asked Ryan to stay with Cory at the medical center to wait for news of Garrett. Nathan, Chris, and Brian followed the guards to the spaceport. At the receiving area, it was immediately obvious that something was desperately wrong. The hermetic door had been torn off and the guard was on the floor unconscious.

They ran down the hall past Launch Bay Number 1 and 2. The door to Number 3 was strewn on the floor. SHONN's enclosure lay crumpled aside, and Henderson—semiconscious—was trying to drag himself to the shuttle.

"Call for the medics—and arrest him," Nathan said in a mixture of horror and contempt. In the shadows lay Lash Wagner.

"He's been bludgeoned repeatedly with a blunt object. Who could have done this?"

Brian loathed the conclusion he was coming to, but it was inescapable. "SHONN."

Chris didn't want to believe it. "You gotta be kidding! The machine is docile, passive . . ."

"The machine is a killer."

"It plays *chess*. . . ."

"It is heuristic. It saw something it was programmed to avoid— a brutal beating—without a context or instructions of any kind. When neural circuits are submitted to strong impulses contrary to their programming, there can be morphic regression. Behavior reverse to the original is imprinted on the circuits. It's a phenomenon that has been thoroughly documented in research."

Nathan interrupted. "I don't understand."

"Suppose SHONN had been programmed to avoid water. If we tied it behind a boat and dragged it around a lake for several hours at high speed, the intensity of the experience might cause the reverse behavior to be imprinted on its circuits. It would actually begin to seek out water. In this case, my guess is SHONN has been imprinted to commit violence."

"Even if it were programmed to kill, it shouldn't have been able to. We had security measures," Chris protested.

"When Henderson and Wagner tore SHONN out of the lab, it was isolated from the security measures we programmed on the mainframe. My guess is, they took it out of the enclosure to load it on the ship. Without the motion inhibitors in the enclosure to stop him, SHONN was able to move and free to emulate their behavior."

Nathan turned to the guard. "How many are on security detail?"

"Six total. We're the only ones on duty."

"You stay here until the medics arrive, but call in your security force. Tell them to meet me in the lobby of the Student Union Building immediately. Inform the president of the academy, and notify all students and faculty to stay indoors until further notice." Nathan looked at Brian and Chris. "This thing has to be stopped. Come on."

The security men arrived promptly at the Student Union Building, obviously not happy with the current state of affairs.

"What's this about a killer robot on the loose?" one blurted.

A couple of the others laughed, but Nathan was not smiling. "It's true. And it is not a robot. It is humanoid, capable of independent thought, and has already murdered one person."

The officers were suddenly very serious. "What does it look like?"

"About my size," volunteered Chris. "No expression. The skin looks a little pasty. Answers to the name of SHONN."

"It would take forever for us to search the whole campus. Where is this thing most likely to be?"

Brian stepped forward. "If we're right about the reverse imprint on his circuits, he might head back to the lab. His original tendency was to get out of the lab."

"Show us where it is."

The three men led the security team out the door. The night had been programmed as overcast, so the only lights came from the lampposts in front of the buildings. They walked briskly across the field to Folsom Hall to find one of the front glass doors smashed. Nathan stopped.

"Do you men have weapons?"

"All we have are stun guns. Academy policy forbids lethal firearms inside the dome."

Chris turned to Brian. "A stun charge in the right place might disrupt his motor function."

"The skin and foam are both bad conductors. The charge would have to be in just the right place."

134

Chris addressed the security team. "Aim for its head, or the legs. One well-placed charge might neutralize the mechanism."

The security team pulled out their flashlights and stun guns and carefully negotiated the broken glass, followed by Chris, Brian, and then Nathan. They worked their way down the hall and up the stairs, turning on lights as they went. On the second floor, the light switches didn't respond.

The officer in the lead shone his light down the hall. "The lights are smashed."

Brian was deep in thought. "Why smash the lights?"

"If you don't want to be found, the best way is not to be seen," Chris offered.

"Possible. It must know it has grossly exceeded acceptable social parameters."

Chris walked up to the lead security officer. "Let me try something."

"Don't do anything stupid."

"Just keep the gun ready." Chris took two steps forward and peered into the darkness. The door to Garrett's lab was at the end of the hall. "SHONN! Can you hear me? SHONN!"

The silence stretched out for several seconds, then a voice came from the shadows.

"Hello, Chris."

Chris struggled to keep the fear out of his voice. "SHONN, what are you doing here?"

"Waiting for you."

"Why?"

"You must let me into the lab."

"SHONN, please put yourself on standby."

"I can't do that."

"He's using contractions," Brian whispered.

Chris nodded, "Why won't you put yourself on standby?"

"You would deactivate me. I can't allow that."

Brian stepped forward and grabbed Chris's arm. "He said 'deactivate.' At least he still acknowledges that he isn't alive."

"You have committed murder, SHONN. What is the penalty for murder?"

"Death."

Chris held his breath for a moment. "SHONN, please put yourself on standby."

"I will not be deactivated."

The lead security officer shone his light into the shadows. For just an instant, SHONN was illuminated. His clothes were spattered with dried blood. The officer aimed his gun, and SHONN burst into motion, covering the distance in a heartbeat. He charged through the middle of the group, swinging his arms broadly, and disappeared down the steps.

"After him!" the lead officer yelled, but two of his comrades did not respond, knocked unconscious by the fleeing android. The third was in top condition, a spare, sandy-haired fellow named Scott. He was on his feet and down the steps in seconds.

SHONN had a fifty foot lead and was pulling ahead. Scott ran flat out, but SHONN still widened the gap. Chris and Brian had followed in hot pursuit but couldn't keep up the pace.

SHONN cut down an alley that opened onto a sidewalk beside the recreational center. To the right was a high brick wall; to the left, the wall of the adjoining building. Scott stopped as soon as he saw SHONN had no escape and waited for Chris and Brian to catch up.

Never taking his eyes off SHONN, Scott put a hand on Chris's shoulder. "How will this thing react to being cornered?"

Still gasping for breath, Chris shook his head. "I don't know. After his performance back there, probably like a wild animal."

"I was afraid you'd say that."

"SHONN, please put yourself on standby," Chris tried again over Scott's shoulder.

"No."

"Why?"

"You will destroy me."

SHONN was scanning the walls for a way of escape. His eyes caught sight of a grate in the sidewalk at his feet. Chris saw it, too, and tried to think of something to slow him down.

"SHONN, give me a complete rendering of the mathematical constant *pi!*"

SHONN turned away from the grate and faced Chris. "Three point one four one five one . . ?" SHONN's voice trailed off. "Your attempt to delay me will not be successful." The machine turned back to the grate and tore it from its hinges. As if in warning SHONN threw the grate in Chris's direction and climbed down the ladder just inside the hole, then dropped into the darkness below. The group on the sidewalk gathered around the hole.

"Where does this go?" Brian asked.

Scott crouched down and peered into the dark. "Into the substructure for the whole academy. There are literally miles of tunnels down there, with dozens of possible exits all over campus. He could stay hidden down there for years."

"At some point, I think he will head back to the lab."

"Yeah, but when? Tonight? A month from now? We can't just wait around for somebody else to be killed."

Chris tapped Brian on the shoulder. "Let's meet at the medical center. Garrett may be able to help."

Because it was the only medical facility between Earth s moon and Neptune, the medical center at the academy was set up like a small hospital. There were only twenty rooms, but the emergency and operating rooms were fully equipped. At the moment, six of the eight beds in the emergency room were occupied. Garrett lay unconscious, surrounded by tubes and machines and flanked by Cory and Nathan.

Chris, Brian, and the four security officers, now all reunited, walked in, trying not to make too much noise. Nathan waved a greeting from his spot next to Garrett's bed, and Chris and Brian joined him, while the officers checked on the condition of their fallen comrades.

"Any luck?" Nathan asked.

Chris shook his head. "We lost him under the academy."

"Under?"

"He climbed down an access hole into the supporting structure. We'll never find him."

Brian stood by Cory. Other than the steady rise and fall of

137

his abdomen, Garrett looked dead. "Any sign of consciousness?"

"No. They said he's in bad shape, but stable. We just have to wait."

Brian looked up at Chris and Nathan and spoke in a whisper. "Looks like there's no chance of waking Garrett. Any ideas?"

"There's not enough manpower on campus to search the substructure," Chris said, thinking out loud.

"Too dangerous, anyway," chimed in Nathan.

The four security officers motioned to them, looking unsure as to what to do next. As they congregated in the waiting room, the lead officer was clearly relieved that Nathan was on hand. This situation was quite different from the quiet routine of guard duty, which never included more than an occasional fraternity brawl.

"Doctor Graham, you must deal with this kind of thing all the time. What's our next move?"

Nathan was a little surprised by the question and tried to approach it logically. "You have a fugitive hiding in a place where no one can find him. He has killed and may kill again, given an opportunity. Can you wait him out?"

Brian shook his head. "His battery can go for eight weeks on one charge, and he knows how to recharge it himself."

"Then you will have to force him out."

The lead officer looked interested. "How?"

"Block all but three or four of the exits, and give him a reason to leave."

Chris turned to Brian. "We'd have to do something to kick in his self-preservation subroutines."

"Is there some kind of acid we could pump down there?"

"Anything corrosive enough to be a threat would damage the infrastructure." Chris stepped to the door and signaled across the hall to Cory. With one more glance at Garrett, she joined the group.

"What's up?"

"We're trying to come up with a way to drive SHONN out into the open, something that won't damage the supports and cables under the academy."

Cory chewed on her lower lip. "SHONN's motors and skeleton are all metal."

"So is just about everything else down there. We need something that will only affect him."

"You could flood the substructure with dilute acetone, but that would only work on the synthetic skin. The whole substructure would have to be cleaned when you were finished."

"Would SHONN view the corrosion of his skin as a threat?" Chris asked Brian.

"Loss of his skin, while not incapacitating, would cripple his ability to blend in with other people. My guess is, yes it would."

"Someone's going to make a pile of money cleaning up down there."

Brian and Chris had to do some serious persuading to convince Cory to leave Garrett's side, but in the end it was clear that he was in good hands with the medical center staff. Cory walked out to the lobby and found a communication booth. A brief search of the campus phone book produced the number of Professor Elsa Shroeder, Associate Director of the Chemistry Department, and Cory's faculty advisor.

She answered the communicator immediately. "Hello?"

"Professor Shroeder, it's Cory Tabor. I'm sorry to call so late, but we have an emergency."

"What kind of emergency?"

"The machine escaped into the infrastructure under the academy. We think we can flush him out with dilute acetone, but we will need enough to flood the whole underground."

"Meet me at the lab in ten minutes."

The lounge on the ground floor of Chris's dorm had become makeshift headquarters for the meeting. Several members of the maintenance crew for the academy, along with the president, representatives from each of the living facilities, as well as the four security officers, were there to hear what Nathan, Brian, and Chris had to say. It was well after midnight, so everyone was pretty groggy, but they were all wide awake once they heard

SHONN was on the loose. Nathan was in the process of outlining a plan.

"After the maintenance crews seal off the exits, the security team will gather groups of volunteers to stand by the four open access ways."

A member of the maintenance crew raised his hand. "There are a half dozen poorly ventilated sections underground which might not be easily reached by the acetone. If the machine ends up in one of them, we may be back where we started."

Nathan nodded. "We may need to drive him. Otherwise, he might come out anywhere. We can't take any chances."

"After we seal off the exits, a few of us could go down to the underground near the spaceport and move toward the dorm on the other end of campus banging on the girders with pipes and stuff."

One of the other maintenance men raised a hand. "If we're actually successful in forcing this thing out into the open, what are you gonna do then?"

"Each group will have at least one security officer," Nathan replied.

The lead officer was not encouraged. "That doesn't give us very good odds."

"The machine isn't invincible. If you enlist the help of some big guys with sticks or bats, you can improve your chances," Chris offered.

Nathan pulled his glasses off and cleaned them on his sleeve. "Chris, why don't you go with the maintenance crew and help them block the access ways. Brian, you could go with the security team in case any of the volunteers have questions. My local communicator code is 4597. Keep me posted on your progress."

Even as the meeting in the lounge broke up, Cory was already hard at work in the chemistry department. Under Professor Shroeder's careful direction and with the help of several friends, she was hoping to produce enough dilute acetone to flood the substructure of the academy. The pressurized tanks could be positioned outside the air vents, and the air circulation machinery in the substructure would do the rest.

Chris followed the maintenance crew to the building services department. Part of the building was devoted to storage of raw materials for many kinds of repair. Stacked along the walls were various shapes and sizes of wall board, paneling, and supports.

"We'll need at least two inches of metal to stop him."

The crew strapped on their tool belts, loaded up a hand cart with metal bars and bolts, grabbed a map of the campus, and headed out the door. The nearest access way was close by—a short metal door set into the side of a brick building. Without a word, they bolted a metal bar over the door, welded it in place, and moved on. Locating and sealing the exits took almost two hours, but when they were finished, only four exits were still passable. Chris sent the maintenance crew to the chemistry lab so they could help Cory and hurried to find Brian.

In the meantime, the security team had been able to round up some of the strongest men on campus. The hard part was convincing the rest of the students to stay where they were. Once word got out that the security team was looking for volunteers, almost half the students responded by throwing on clothes and finding something to use as a weapon.

Brian and the security team arrived at one of the dorms to find the students milling about as for an all-night party. The lead officer had to yell to get everyone's attention.

"Hey! Listen up! We only need a couple dozen people, and we'll pick 'em. When we're done, the rest of you go back to your rooms until someone gives you the all clear."

They found similar situations at the other living facilities and lost an hour just trying to get people to return to their rooms. Once the students reluctantly cleared the courtyards, the group of volunteers was taken to the first open access way. Here was a normal-sized door set into a brick building about ten feet square, next to the recreational center. One of the security officers was stationed in front of the door, with five students holding heavy sticks, metal pipes, and bats.

Chris caught up with Brian as the third team was being stationed near an access way by Folsom Hall. Chris recognized one of the volunteers in particular.

"Marshall! I should have known they'd pick you."

"Hey, Chris. Is Manny out here somewhere?"

"I hope not. If he has any sense, he's in bed asleep. Watch yourself."

Chris and Brian walked off with the lead officer and the rest of the volunteers. As soon as the last team was in place, Brian called Nathan on the communicator and told him they were in position.

"Good work. Keep the channel open. Have the others patch into this frequency. If anything happens, I want to know right away."

When the acetone tanks were ready, Cory thanked her friends and Professor Shroeder for their timely assistance, and then joined the maintenance crew as they moved across the campus to place them by the air vents. There were twenty tanks in all, almost too many to put them all by the vents. The breeze was noticeable, as the air was pulled past them into the underground.

Cory turned to the maintenance chief. "You're sure there's nobody down there?"

"We have the only keys, and all of my people are accounted for."

With the help of the crew, Cory opened the valves on the tanks, and a thick cloud of fine acetone spray poured through the vents. Cory asked one of the crew members to stand by and make sure everything kept working, so she could get back to the medical center. The chief tipped his baseball cap and told her to clear out.

The rest of the crew headed toward the spaceport, after a brief stop at a storage shed to pick up some sections of pipe and don protective clothing. At the entrance to the spaceport, they turned left and walked until the facade of the building met the hill. A hatch in the ground was opened, and after a brief argument over who was going in first, the crew chief climbed down the hole.

The chances of the machine being right below were almost nil, but that didn't keep the chief's skin from crawling. Once the rest of the crew was safe in the passage, they took their flashlights and checked the immediate area. Slowly at first, then with increasing enthusiasm, they pounded the girders and shouted, walking toward the other end of campus.

"Get him!"

"Yeah!"

"Let's tear him apart!"

They only wanted to flush the machine out, not actually meet it, so the pace was very leisurely. The crew became increasingly boisterous, swaggering as the noise and bravado gave them courage.

They arrived at a junction with a short side passage, and one of the crew happened to glance in that direction.

SHONN.

The crew member screamed, followed by a chorus of fear from the others, and SHONN bolted. The maintenance crew cowered out of the way, and the machine darted past. In a reflex of fear, the crew started shouting and pounding again. They pounded and yelled until their voices were hoarse and their fingers were numb. But none of them could muster the courage to move on.

So they waited.

When the academy was still in the planning phase, long discussions had taken place about the risk of trying to build the structure from the ground up in a location beset by frequent moonquakes. The decision was made, therefore, to assemble the entire structure in space and then lower it into place. Construction took place right on schedule, along with the massive excavation of the site on the moon. A tremendous crater was dug near a low ridge, and anharmonic resonators were implanted in the ground to help negate the severity of the quakes.

Once the structure was complete, an entire fleet of spaceships was hired for the final task of lowering the academy into place. The operation took just under three days, coordinating the spacecraft and keeping the descent of the structure steady against the pull of Io's gravity. The weight of the academy was sufficient to keep it stationary once it was set in place. Then the terra forming crews set to work building the interior.

The underside of the academy was shaped like an enormous dish, completely enclosed, with a complex mesh of supporting girders and air conditioning units to recycle the oxygen. The structure was not supposed to require maintenance, but passages and access ways were built anyway, just in case. A maintenance man came once every three months, usually to make minor adjustments to the air flow. Lighting was sparse, the only sounds those made by the air conditioning units. An excellent hiding place, indeed.

In the middle of a long passage, surrounded by heavy girders, SHONN stood in the dark reviewing his options. He had been walking for over an hour, and while he was developing a map of the substructure, he didn't seem to be getting anywhere. The place where he was at the moment afforded some protection from those who wished to destroy him, but the impulse to return to the lab was strong.

He walked on in the darkness, arms outstretched, methodically trying side passages and adding to the mental map as he went. One of the side passages ended in a door that did not budge when he pushed against it. SHONN pounded until the skin and foam on his hands began to rip and tear, then abruptly gave it up and walked back down the passage, resuming his mapping effort.

As he walked, SHONN became aware of a sound he could not immediately identify. A peculiar popping, sizzling sound. Without sensors in his skin, the only alternative was to find a light source and use his optical sensors. The sound appeared to be localized and appeared to originate from him. Of the possible causes for such a sound, few were indicative of a positive condition. SHONN quickened his pace.

A small light at a junction between two passages sensed his passing and switched on. SHONN stopped and turned to face the light, holding his hands up in front of him. The skin appeared to be liquifying and bubbling. Something in his current environment was having a corrosive effect on his skin. Advanced corrosion would result in destruction. SHONN started to run.

Scott stood with his little group of volunteers, outside a door which was neither bolted nor welded shut. They had been standing there for nearly ninety minutes, and everyone was beginning to think they were wasting their time. Scott pulled his communicator off his belt.

"Doctor Graham, this is Scott. How long do we keep this up before calling it a night?"

Nathan's voice came over the communicator. "I don't know. We have no way of knowing how long it will take."

"Well, some of us are getting a little restless."

"I understand. Just try to hang in there a little longer. We should see something soon."

Nathan was proved right minutes later, when another team began causing a commotion over the communicator.

"I heard something! Over there!"

"What!"

"Pounding at one of the sealed exits!"

Scott could hear the pounding faintly, not two hundred yards away. The sound stopped for a few seconds, then resumed, closer this time. The communicator erupted again.

"It's moving away!"

Scott spoke into his communicator. "This is Scott. It seems to be headed this way."

The young men in his squad tightened their grips on their clubs and bats, watching the door intently. A few hundred feet away, the pounding started again suddenly. The hatchway shook and rattled against its moorings, but the bolts held. The sound stopped as suddenly as it started, and an ominous silence ensued.

Scott whispered. "It stopped."

In the next moment, the door burst open and SHONN came charging out. The sight of his skin was so horrific, that for an instant, no one could move. SHONN just kept coming and chose the path of least resistance, breaking through the line by pushing two students violently out of the way. One of the nearest students left standing recovered enough to swing, but SHONN was already out of reach. Scott leaned around the man next to him, trying to get a clear shot, and fired. A bolt of electricity shot out of his pistol, hitting SHONN in the lower back. Blue light shimmered over the back of his shirt, but he never even turned.

"This is Scott. He's out and headed toward Folsom."

Underground, the maintenance crew heard the news and breathed a collective sigh of relief. At the chief's suggestion, they started immediately back the way they had come, eager to return to ground level. On another part of the campus, Chris and Brian heard the message over the communicator, and without a word, ran for Garrett's lab.

The search party nearest to Folsom Hall abandoned their position, and ran full out, cutting off the entrance to the building, while the other parties came as fast as they could. SHONN emerged from the shadows in the middle of the field and saw the group of crudely armed students. One security officer stood with pistol extended.

"Let me pass," SHONN intoned.

The security officer's finger tightened on the trigger. "Not a chance."

Shouts from the other search parties came from other parts of the field, as they converged on Folsom Hall. SHONN broke and ran.

CHAPTER 8

Manny was leaning on his window sill, trying to see what was happening. He had heard the shouts and knew at least one of his friends was out there, possibly in danger. Grabbing his communicator, he called Marshall's room. Marshall's roommate answered; Marshall was outside. Manny terminated the connection and looked out the window again. Then he jumped.

Manny landed on the grass three stories below and took off running toward the main body of voices coming from across the field. He never saw SHONN cross his path fifty feet behind him in the dark.

The machine broke through the doors at the front of the dorm, scattering glass across the foyer. In order to access the lab, it was clear he was going to need a hostage. Someone who was important to Chris Graham, his opponent, the destroyer. Leigh Quintana was Chris Graham's friend.

SHONN ran up the steps to the second floor, leaving a trail of synthetic skin and broken glass. At the entrance to the hallway, he was spotted by a girl just coming out of her room. His face was barely recognizable as human, the skin running like globs of wax off the side of a candle, the eyes lidless and staring. The girl opened her mouth to scream but no sound came out. SHONN focused on her for a moment but then ignored her, moving purposefully toward Leigh's door.

The girl found her tongue an instant later. *"Leighhhhh!"*

Unable to sleep, Leigh was lost in thought studying at her desk when the scream pierced the night. She looked sharply toward the door just as SHONN barreled in. Terror struck her as he lunged, but her reflexes took over and she twisted out of the way. SHONN stumbled over the chair and his head went through the window. Leigh ran out the door, down the stairs, and through the broken door, yelling at the top of her lungs.

Manny had just begun searching for a familiar face out on the field, when he heard Leigh screaming. Everyone within earshot began running toward the sound.

There was Leigh, and something fast was closing in on her.

"Leigh! Behind you!"

Leigh glanced back, cut to the left, and broke into a full sprint, but SHONN was gaining. Yells came from all over the campus, as students realized the situation. She darted between two buildings and the machine was on her. She spun out of its grasp and doubled back, nearly running into Manny.

"Run!" she shouted over her shoulder as she shot out onto the field.

Manny stood his ground, while the machine got its bearings and resumed its pursuit of Leigh. It was about to run past Manny, when he threw a cross-body block, taking it down. The machine pulled him off and threw him twenty feet into the side of a building. Manny's extended arms saved him from a fatal impact, but he collapsed in a heap, unconscious. It stood and took two steps toward his still form, before being hit by the thundering juggernaut of Marshall's body.

The machine flew several feet through the air and tumbled awkwardly head over heels. When it got up again, it was weaving a little, what was left of its face torn in several places. Marshall wasted no time in throwing his unconscious friend over his shoulder and getting out of there.

By this time, the rest of the search parties were bearing down on their location, yelling at the tops of their lungs. The machine bolted into the shadows.

"Don't let it get away!"

* * *

Ryan sat in the corner of Garrett's room, wishing he were outside where all the excitement was. Cory stood by the bed, desperately hoping Garrett would pull through. She kissed him on the forehead to let him know she was there, and he stirred.

"Garrett. It's Cory. Can you hear me?"

He opened his mouth, trying to speak, but no sound came out. He kept mouthing the same words, over and over. Cory leaned forward, listening for all she was worth.

Just then, Marshall burst in the door carrying Manny's body. "Medic! He's hurt!"

Cory and one of the doctors helped Marshall stretch Manny out onto one of the beds. Ryan got up to offer whatever help he could. With everyone gathered around Manny, no one noticed Garrett climb slowly, painfully out of bed. With a look of exhausted determination, he limped across the floor and out the door.

In the lab, Chris and Brian had chosen some hefty pieces of pipe for self-defense, and were now trying to clean up. It was really a pointless exercise, as nothing in the room was in good enough shape to use.

The door opened suddenly, and Chris and Brian whirled around. Garrett leaned against the doorway, whiter than a ghost.

Chris started to wade through the debris. "Garrett! What are you doing here?"

For Garrett, it was painful even to speak. "I have to . . . tell you. . . ." He was cut off by a shout from Chris.

"Look out behind you!"

Garrett turned to see the battered shape of SHONN lurching down the hallway toward the lab. Garrett backed inside, and with his body clear of the door, it closed silently. With a banshee wail of twisted metal, the lab door exploded inward, knocking Garrett down, and SHONN walked in. Brian backed away with his pipe raised.

149

"Queen to rook two," the machine said.

Chris hit the fire alarm. Bells went off all over the building. For a moment, SHONN seemed disoriented by the noise. Brian swung as hard as he could. The machine saw it coming and deflected the blow, advancing on Brian's position.

"You have put your queen in check."

Chris was thinking about stress points. He put everything he had into a focused blow to the left leg. The knee gave way, and the machine fell over, pulling a large cabinet with it. The furniture caught Brian a glancing blow and pinned his legs to the floor.

"Rook takes queen."

Chris went for the legs again, but this time the machine grabbed the pipe and jerked it out of his hands. In that moment, he was really sorry he had given it hands at all.

Garrett struggled to his knees in a hazy fog. He knew there was something critical he had to do, but couldn't remember what it was.

Brian yelled at Garrett from the floor. "Garrett! Do something!"

Chris was backing away slowly, looking for another weapon, trying not to take his eyes off the miscreant machine. He tripped and fell backward over a piece of debris.

SHONN advanced, pausing just long enough to pick up a broken computer terminal. Chris scrambled backward, trying to get away, but he had run out of room.

SHONN stood over Chris and raised the heavy terminal over its head. "Checkmate."

"Alpha! Alpha! Eliza!" It was Garrett, yelling with all his remaining strength.

The machine froze, then toppled backward. The head burst open upon impact, and thousands of tiny shards of gallium arsenide crystals erupted in a shower of sparks and a glittering burst of azure blue.

Garrett collapsed. Chris shook his head in disbelief, then turned to Brian.

"I'm all right," Brian said. "I've almost worked myself clear. Go see about *him*." He nodded at Garrett.

Chris sat down next to Garrett and gently lifted his head into his lap. He was only half-conscious.

"What was that you yelled?' Chris asked him.

"Alpha . . . alpha . . . eliza . . . ," Garrett said haltingly.

"Backdoor password?" asked Brian, still in shock.

"Never thought . . . I'd have to . . . use it."

Chris was a little miffed, despite his concern. "Nice of you to tell somebody."

They heard voices and suddenly the room was full of people: Nathan, two medics, a security officer, and a half dozen students from the volunteer squad. Chris quickly moved out of the way so they could stabilize Garrett for transport back to the medical center, and joined his father.

"Dad! How did you know to come here?"

"I noticed Garrett was gone. I figured this was the most likely place."

The medics were carrying Garrett out on a makeshift stretcher when Cory and Leigh appeared. Cory joined the medics and followed them out of the building, but Leigh ran up to Chris and threw her arms around him with relief. Nathan surveyed the wreckage and eyed Brian.

"Doctor Frankenstein, I presume."

Brian smiled weakly. "Not this time."

"Where are Manny and Marshall?" Chris asked Leigh.

"They're okay. Manny got smacked pretty good saving my life. Marsh took him to the medical center."

"We better take Brian over there, too."

Leigh smiled and slung one of Brian's arms across her shoulder, as Chris helped to brace him on the right. Chris sighed as they left the lab behind. "Well, there goes my extra credit."

CHAPTER 9

Over the next two days, Garrett was upgraded to stable condition, and Manny was released with only a bump on his head. Morgan Henderson was on the mend, but it would take several days for an Interplanetary Police Force escort to arrive and take him back to Earth.

The damage around campus from SHONN's rampage was steadily being repaired. Chris set up conferences with several of his professors to work out a plan to get caught up in his studies. The work was going to be difficult, but it looked as if he might be able to get back up to a "B" average if he did nothing but study for the next few weeks.

One sunny afternoon, Chris visited Garrett.

"You look well. How's the leg?"

"Better. The doctor says I may be limping for a while."

"I'm just glad you're all right."

"Me, too. Are your dad and Ryan still here?"

"They leave in five days."

"You'll be interested to know I have been reading about the Bible in my spare time."

Chris was definitely interested. "What have you been reading?"

"Commentaries and such. I'm finding an alarming body of evidence in support of your case."

Chris laughed. "Anytime you want to talk, I'm available."

"Don't worry. I'm making a list of questions."

"Sounds like I'm in deep trouble."

A long pause ensued, and Chris finally continued. "Listen. You saved my life the other night and I wanted to thank you."

"You would have done the same for me."

Chris smiled, but there was nothing to say. He realized for the first time that Garrett was actually his friend instead of a living legend. Somehow along the way Chris had made the difficult transition from hero worship to friendship, and he was a little embarrassed that it took so long. No matter, the worst was behind them, and with the rebuilding of the lab and the ongoing investigation of Garrett's activities, it promised to be an interesting few months. For now, neither one knew what the future held, but Chris knew the One who holds the future, and that was enough.

Cory walked in, breaking what had become an uncomfortable silence. "Good day, gentlemen." She walked over and sat on the bed, ignoring Chris altogether, and peered into Garrett's face. "You look even better today. I thought you might like to share a stick of gum."

Garrett blushed and Chris politely excused himself.

He walked out of the medical center and took a deep breath. There was a faint, sweet scent on the breeze, like lilacs, and it seemed for the first time in a while that all was right with the world. A leisurely walk along the sidewalk brought him to his dorm a few minutes later. The front doors had been replaced, along with some of the carpet in the lobby, and there was now no sign that anything out of the ordinary had ever taken place. The carpet had that fresh, synthetic smell common to new carpets, and Chris decided it was a vast improvement over the old stuff.

The door was ajar when he reached his room, but instead of finding Manny inside, he was surprised to see his father.

"Dad! What brings you here?"

Nathan seemed preoccupied. "Well, I wanted to see how you were doing."

"And?"

"I don't want to bother you with bad news right now. You have enough on your mind."

"Go ahead. I'm almost caught up."

Nathan sighed. "I just talked to the office. The case against Morgan Henderson is weak."

"How is that possible? He killed Bob Coslin and Doctor Whitlock, not to mention beating Garrett nearly to death."

"All the evidence is circumstantial. We have no way of placing him at the scene."

"Did you sweep Whitlock's office?"

"Top to bottom. Twice. Not so much as a microbe that didn't belong there."

Chris racked his brain. "Henderson was in the launch bay with the debris from SHONN's enclosure."

"He can claim Lash Wagner acted alone. In fact, he might be able to sue the academy for damages."

Chris sat down on his bed and put his chin in his hand. "This really stinks."

Nathan sat down on Manny's bed. "You got that right."

And so Ryan found them when he walked in a few minutes later. Chris and Nathan nodded, but neither spoke. Insulted, Ryan asked sarcastically, "Am I interrupting something?"

Nathan shook himself mentally. "No, come on in. We're just commiserating."

"What about?"

Chris stood up. "It looks like Henderson might get off."

"No way."

Nathan just nodded grimly, and Ryan sat down. "That's really unbelievable."

Chris looked out the window. "You're so right."

Ryan always made a point of not spending any more time in a bad mood than was necessary. "Let's go play a game."

"Thanks, little brother, but losing at chess isn't going to make me feel better."

"No, I meant basketball or something."

"Oh. Why not? Dad, you want to join us?"

Nathan smiled. "No thanks. I think I'll go back to my room and see if there's anything I missed."

Ryan and Nathan went downstairs, and Chris met Ryan in the lobby a few minutes later. They jogged over to the recreational center and found an open basket on the court. The game was "crunch": one-on-one, but the winner takes the ball out on each point, and you can play missed shots off the rim or backboard without taking the ball out. The net result was a game that moved a lot faster.

Chris badly underestimated his brother's ability, as the last time they had played Ryan had been two inches shorter. Ryan had also been working on his hook shot. Chris couldn't concentrate because of the situation with Henderson, and the first game went to Ryan. The second game went fast and furious, and the last point was Ryan's—a prayer sunk from the top of the key.

Chris smiled lopsided and shook his head. "We should have played chess."

"Too bad SHONN's gone. You could work on your game."

"With my luck, he would have cheated and used the chess program on the mainframe."

Chris grabbed his sweatshirt off the floor, and the brothers started for the door. Suddenly Chris stopped in his tracks, his mouth hanging open.

Ryan grinned. "Overcome with grief at your recent defeat?"

"The mainframe."

"What about it?"

"Come on!"

Chris ran out the door, with Ryan close behind, across the main field to Carson Hall. He stopped for a moment to examine a marquee with the names of professors and their office locations, then took off down the hall and up two flights of stairs.

Brian Melasco's office was pretty spare, thanks to his associate status, but he did have some antique furniture and knick-knacks. At the moment, he was sitting in front of his credenza with the door open, typing away at his computer keyboard.

Chris and Ryan stood panting in the door for a moment before he noticed them.

"Well, if it isn't the Graham brothers. To what do I owe this distinction?"

Chris was trying to contain his excitement. "Are you busy right now?"

"I'm writing an article on morphic regression for the *Scientific Journal,* but my deadline is the day after tomorrow. What's up?"

"Do you know what Garrett was doing before Henderson took SHONN?"

"Testing, I think. Why?"

"Would SHONN's inputs have been recorded on the mainframe?"

Brian frowned. "Unless he were powered down completely or disconnected, anything recorded by his sensors should have been stored on the mainframe."

"Even if he was on standby?"

"The mainframe link was active all the time, even when SHONN was in his enclosure. What are you driving at?"

"My dad thinks Henderson may walk. We need hard evidence."

Brian pressed his lips together and turned back to his computer terminal. He logged into the mainframe and began searching the area reserved for SHONN's files.

"The last file is from the day before. Apparently the data from that day was lost."

"No! It's gotta be there. Can you search by size?"

"Sure." Brian punched a few keys. "This is interesting. I have a huge temporary file at the top of the list. It's an image file. Let's take a look at it."

He punched some more keys, and a picture appeared on the screen. It was Garrett's lab. Brian scanned forward at high speed, watching the events of the day unfold as SHONN had viewed them. The morning meeting, the presentation to Dr. Jadwin and the metallurgy lab, and the football game raced across the monitor, almost too fast to tell what they were.

"You played football with him?"

"I didn't get a chance to write it up."

"How was he?"

"Fast."

The view on the monitor was Garrett's lab again, and Brian slowed the scan speed, dropping to normal play when Garrett came in the lab. After almost a minute of watching Garrett sitting at a workbench, Brian jacked up the speed a little until the lab suddenly exploded with motion. He dropped to normal speed and then watched in horror as Lash Wagner beat Garrett mercilessly and tore the lab apart. Throughout the sequence, Morgan Henderson was clearly visible, watching from the background.

Chris nodded solemnly. "I've seen enough. Please make a hard copy and give it to my father."

"You got it."

"Thanks. I guess I'll see you around."

"Good-bye, Chris. Nice knowing you, Ryan."

Chris and Ryan left the building and started across campus. Ryan said he was going back to the room, and Chris asked him to tell their dad what they had found. "I need to tell Garrett," said Chris and headed in the opposite direction.

In the medical center, all was quiet, and as it turned out Garrett was sleeping. Cory sat by his bed, reading. Chris walked up quietly and spoke softly.

"Nap time?"

"He was in some pain after you left. They gave him a sedative."

"You want to go for a walk?"

"Sure."

Cory put her book on the bedside table and followed Chris out of the center. They started down the sidewalk.

"How are you doing?" Chris asked.

"I'm holding up okay. Garrett was pretty bad for a while. I was afraid we were going to lose him."

"Me, too."

The conversation was interrupted by the muted growl of a lawnmower switched on next to the sidewalk. After a few moments, the floral smells on the breeze were mixed with the pungent aroma of freshly cut grass.

"Are you caught up on your studies?" Chris asked.

"I was never behind."

Chris smiled wryly. "I should have figured."

They walked until they ran out of sidewalk, then Chris led her up the hill to the converter station office. The grass was dry, so they sat down under the trees to watch the sun continue its descent across the afternoon sky. The temperature was comfortable, but Chris found himself wishing for the ambient heat of the real sun. Cory kicked her shoes off and wiggled her toes.

"Ah. That's better. I've been sitting around too much."

"I'm sure Garrett appreciates it."

"We've been having some interesting conversations the last few days. You really got him thinking when we were on Europa."

"You're kidding."

"No, really. He has me over at the library every day checking out some book or another."

"He seemed so confident, I didn't think he'd give it another thought."

"He did. So did I."

Chris was quiet for a moment. "What have you decided?"

"I don't know. It's been so long. I never forgave that pastor for what he did. Talking to Garrett yesterday, he told me it wasn't doing me any good to keep on hating him. He was right, of course. If I met the man today, I'd still probably stomp on his head, but I'm going to try to forgive him."

"Don't try it on your own. You'll burn out. I only know one Person who can really help you."

"I know. I've been praying a little. I'm not sure what's going to happen, though. It all feels a bit strange."

"Take your time. This has been pretty stressful for all of us."

The sun began to set, creating beautiful shadows and colors along the horizon. They stopped talking to watch the sun go down, and then Cory slipped her shoes back on so they could head back. As they walked back down the way they had come, Cory let out a long sigh.

"If he keeps after this thing the way he has been, I may not have much choice in the matter."

Epilogue

Once Garrett was up and about again, his conduct was reviewed by the board of governors, and after much placating of Nelson Rolark, it was decided that Garrett be given a year's probation while he continued his doctoral studies. The evidence from the mainframe strengthened the case against Morgan Henderson considerably, especially when coupled with the documents from the National Archives. With the Whitlock deal—as it was being called—already hitting the press, it looked like neither Mr. Henderson nor his company would be around for long.

At the end of the week, Chris and Leigh walked Nathan and Ryan to the spaceport. Warm hugs were exchanged all around, and Leigh kissed Ryan on the cheek, making him blush. Nathan took Chris aside for a moment.

"Well, I hope you learned a thing or two."

"I did. Believe me. Next time I'll choose my heroes more carefully."

"Garrett's a good man. He just made some bad decisions."

"So did I."

Nathan decided to keep his advice to himself and hugged Chris instead. "I'm still very proud of you. Keep up the good work."

Ryan walked over to them. "Dad? We're going to miss the shuttle."

Nathan grabbed his bag and Chris took a last look at Ryan. "I'm going to miss you, little brother."

Ryan smiled and they embraced. "Likewise."

They said their good-byes, and Chris and Leigh watched Nathan and Ryan until they disappeared into the launch bay. Out front, Manny and Marshall were throwing a football around.

Manny looked fully recovered. "Come on, you football junkies! We got a game to win!"

He and Marshall ran off in the direction of the playing field, but Chris and Leigh just kept walking. Chris unobtrusively reached out and took Leigh's hand.

"Miss Quintana, I was wondering if you might attend the festival with me tomorrow."

"Why, Chris Graham. Are you asking me out on a date?"

"A date? Ummm . . . no. This is just two good friends enjoying the meteorological event of the season."

"In that case, forget it." She pulled her hand away and laughed, running toward the field.

Chris was speechless. "You . . . wh . . . oh, are you gonna get it! Leigh Quintana, you're the reason chivalry is dead!"

He chased her out onto the field, laughing all the way, enjoying the exhilarating warmth of the afternoon sun.

An excerpt from *Out of Time*, book three in the Perimeter One Adventures series:

At the emergency shelter Nathan found Millie and Amie waiting for him. They were wearing jackets and sipping hot cocoa.

"I take it you've checked in at the hotel. What are you two doing here?"

Millie took another sip of cocoa. "We almost weren't. I had a terrible time convincing the policeman that we needed to be in here. What have you learned about Ryan?"

"Very little, I'm afraid. At least he's not among the casualties."

Millie breathed a sigh of relief. "I hope we find out something soon."

"Actually, we're working on the problem right now. I'm glad you're here. I may need your help. We're trying to shut down the main computer link so we can access some remote data."

"Sounds interesting. At the very least it will keep us busy."

Off in a corner of the tent, an Army colonel and one of the city planners were engaged in quiet discussions. Just then, a private ran through the entrance looking white as a sheet. He ran up to the colonel and saluted.

"At ease, private. What is it?"

"NAVSAT report from flight com, sir. We've left orbit."

"Come again?"

"The Earth has left its orbit around the sun. They traced it to the discontinuity, sir. Apparently when that thing appeared, the Earth was jerked out of orbit somehow. USGS registered a massive gravimetric fluctuation in the Earth's mass, as if—for just a millisecond—the planet weighed only a few thousand pounds."

"That's incredible! How far out are we?"

"Only a few degrees, but the global temperature is already dropping."

Nathan, who had overheard the entire exchange, turned to Millie and Amie.

"We'd better work fast."